D1526353

I CAN'T SLEEP

j.e. rowney

Copyright © 2020 JE Rowney

This is a work of fiction. Names, characters,
businesses, places, events, locales, and incidents
are either the products of the author's
imagination or used in a fictitious manner. Any
resemblance to actual persons, living or dead, or
actual events is purely coincidental.

ISBN: 9798612670131

Chapter One

It wasn't always like this. Once I could fall asleep anywhere at any time. Once I could head for an early night, take a good book to read, intend to finish a chapter and wake up the next morning with my face on the page and my book light still glaring. Once I could sleep through a whole series of alarms, only to be woken by my mum shaking me, telling me that I was late for school. If you are able to sleep, you take it for granted. It's a physiological process. It just happens. Living without sleep is hell. Try it.

When did it start? Friday 16th June 2018. Yes, I remember the date. I remember everything about that day. That night. Believe me, I would rather not. I would rather none of it ever happened, but it did. Ever since then, I haven't been able to sleep. It's impossible to exist without sleep. Exist. I guess that's what I have been doing. What I mean is, humans need sleep to live. I live on, exist on, the bare minimum. The brief snatches where I close my eyes, long blinks. Nothing more.

Somehow, I managed to pass my exams. Somehow. Despite everything, perhaps to spite everything. To prove to myself that what happened wasn't going to stop me from living my life. To prove to everyone else that...that what happened wasn't for nothing. I don't want to talk about that yet. We'll get to it. I promise.

Anyway, I passed my exams, and amazingly I did well enough to land a place here at Wessex University. I would say that I have always wanted to be a journalist, but I actually spent several years dreaming of being a psychologist. Ironic, really. After what happened, I couldn't bear thinking about it. I only stopped seeing my therapist just before I came to uni. So, about three weeks ago. I don't think I was ready. I still need help. I know that now.

I'm lying on my bed in my dorm room. They have this cute way of decorating them, so they look like sterile cells. The walls are bricks, painted white, not even plastered. There's two floor-to-ceiling windows with grimy-looking grey curtains that are actually clean. I have a desk that folds down from the wall and a bookshelf that I've filled with my extensive paperback collection. There are no textbooks on there. Everything is available as digital download, ebook, online reference now. Oh, and there's a block-like bedside cabinet. I keep my meds in there; whatever they are currently trying me on. I also have a bottle of Jack Daniels, lying on its side, label up. On top of the drawers is my alarm clock. It's one of those old-fashioned analogue types, with the big silver bells on top. It's an ornament more than anything else. A keepsake, a memento. It was a gift from my brother, in the time before.

"Becky!"

There's an insistent hammering on my door.

The clock tells me it's ten to one. I have a lecture in ten minutes.

"Okay," I shout back, in acknowledgement.

Our "dorms" are four-bedroom flats. There are two sets of four on this floor, two down below. Three identical blocks border a bland concrete square. I live in South Block. They didn't even take the time to give it an interesting name.

I share my flat with two other girls and one boy. I'm eighteen, I don't mind still being called a *girl*. It's how I think of myself. They're all the same age as me, all freshers. Coincidentally Cally shares some modules with me, so she's acting in the role of my PA today.

"Becky, come on. Let's go."

Cally won't give up until I get up and get to the door. I may not be able to sleep, but I am pretty good at lounging around on my bed doing nothing. I think she sees me as some kind of a pet project. Or maybe as some kind of a pet, I haven't decided yet. Much as I don't mind being a girl, I also don't mind a bit of mollycoddling. I don't find it patronising or suffocating. I appreciate her caring. The person I was in the time before fought against all of that. I pushed people away. Now, I want to fit in, I want to belong, I want people to care about me.

I pull myself up to my feet, drag a brush through my curly blonde mess of hair, and tug on my boots.

"Coming. I really am coming, hang on." I speak just loudly enough for her to hear me and stop knocking.

My bag is on the floor, where I dropped it after yesterday's lectures. I scoop it up and pull the door open.

"You look like shit," Cally says. I usually do. If I haven't mentioned it, I can't sleep.

"You too," I say. She doesn't. She looks like she spent the last hour getting ready. Her black, bobbed hair is shiny and sleek. Her make-up is perfect. She probably learned her skills from some YouTube blogger. My make-up skills are self-taught, which basically means I dab it on with my fingers and hope for the best. If I wear any at all, that is, and mostly I can't be bothered.

"I could sort out your bags for you if we had time." She points at the dark circles under my eyes then looks at her watch. I know it must be five to already. We certainly don't have time for makeovers.

"They give me character." I attempt a smile. Maybe I should pay more attention to making better of myself. Maybe I've just stopped giving a shit.

Cally is on the BA English course, but today's class, Creative Non-Fiction, is on the syllabus for both that and my BA Journalism. It's a big group, and I appreciate that. Today I am ready to sit at the back and participate as little as possible.

We make our way down the path between South and West, towards the main square of the campus. All the lecture theatres and classrooms are arranged in the blocks around Main. Just beyond here is the Student Union building. I spend more time there than I do in lectures, but that's partly because I'm only timetabled for five classes a week.

Cally's talking to me about something she's seen on Facebook. Something about a television programme I've never seen. I make the right noises at the right time, but I'm out of touch. I don't watch television, I don't see movies, I have no idea about what's *cool*.

We walk as quickly as we can without running. Our lecturer is pretty laid back, but being late means having to sit at the front, and neither of us want that. Cally loves her mobile phone too much. Tapping away in class seems far less impolite when you're not in direct view of the teacher. Clearly, we should have set off earlier, because when I open the classroom door the only seats left are right at the front. I should ask Cally to call for me earlier. Maybe I should take responsibility for myself.

Cally looks at me and rolls her eyes and I give her a shrug and turn my lips down in reply. She shuffles along the seats behind the long straight desk. We are in rows, stepping up in height, like a theatre. I remember that it's called a lecture theatre and my concentration on the class is already slipping.

I start to think about the other kinds of theatre. The one for plays. The one for operations. The theatre that I was in. Suddenly I'm back there, the whole scene flashing through my mind like a movie on fast forward. White sheets. Gowned doctors. Blood. Noise. Muffled noise. Something banging against my leg.

"Hey. It's a bit soon for that," Cally whispers loudly into my ear.

The banging on my leg was a swift kick. I had slipped into a micro-sleep. These are the only sleeps I have. I'm not certain that they help me, but I don't want to give them up.
I nod in her direction and smile. I haven't even got my laptop out yet. That's probably a record for me.

I look up towards the lecturer, and see she is fiddling with the computer, trying to get something to work. I guess she didn't see me slip away there.

I wriggle in my seat, reach into my bag, and get ready to pay attention. I can do this. No matter what has happened. I can make a life. I can be a good student. I can be all the things that Jordan couldn't. Jordan. Every time I think his name I choke up. Still. Two years later. Maybe I always will.

Chapter Two

I registered at the health centre before I enrolled for my classes. My insomnia controls everything I do, everything I don't do. I don't want to be defined by it, but it's hard not to be. Sleeplessness is a slow torture.

I wanted to get it over with, if I'm honest. I knew that when I went to see the doctor, I would have to go over everything again. Every time I see another professional, I have to tell the whole story. Talking about it doesn't make things any better. It usually makes it worse.

I heard about this place where they flooded a village, made a reservoir out of the area where it had been. I feel like that. Like I've tried to wash out everything that hurts to think about. Drown it. Sometimes the water level drops, sometimes it gets so hot that the tops of the buildings start to show. Sometimes I could walk right into them, kick off my boots and take a seat in those fucking houses. Talking about it drains me. In every sense.

"Rebecca Braithwaite," I said, leaning through the little window where the receptionist was sitting, drinking tea from a mug emblazoned with the caption "Don't talk to me before I've had my coffee!".

"Okay," she said, tapping into the computer, not looking up. "Flat Three, South Block?"

"That's the one."

"Take a seat. Doctor is running to schedule today. Shouldn't be long."

Running to schedule. She had to tell me that because it's such a unique situation these days. You expect to wait in a waiting room. It's in the name. That's the very purpose of the room. Sit and wait.

The doctor swivelled towards me and smiled. She was younger than I expected. I always think of GPs as older. I guess I still think of them as men. Doctor Sally Fisher was neither. Is neither. She's still my doctor. It's been three weeks; she hasn't had time to ditch me yet.

I smiled back, awkwardly, my nerves already starting to bubble in my throat.

"Take a seat, Miss Braithwaite."

"Becky," I said. "I dare say we will be seeing a lot of each other so you might as well call me Becky."

Then it was her turn to look awkward. Maybe most patients don't arrive with the intention of being regular customers.

"Okay. What can I do for you, Becky?"

I came out with it. "I've had insomnia for the past two years. I have a list of the drugs that I've been on. I wasn't sure if you'd have my notes yet?" I pulled the paper out of my bag and handed it across to her.

"Everything is on the computer system," she said.

She took the note off me anyway and gave it a cursory glance. Of course, it would be on the system. I wasted my time writing that out. I knew then that I had highlighted myself as *one of those patients*. The type that think they know everything. The type that obsess about their own condition. The type that make lists for their doctor. I realised that I was sitting in silence, and that I probably looked like an idiot. I think a lot about what other people think. Apart from when I don't. Sometimes I don't think about that at all.

"Two years," she repeated, and I nodded. "That sounds pretty tough going. Do you want to tell me a bit about that? How it started? How it affects you?"

Not really.

"Yeah," I said. I looked down at my boots and tried to remember how I usually started the story. Once upon a time there was a girl called Rebecca Braithwaite.

I didn't say that. I clammed up. My mouth sealed shut, dry, broken.

"Take your time," she said in a way that made me feel hurried.

"Something bad happened. There was a...a *trigger event*."

She nodded, encouragingly.

I told her the most compact version of the events that I could. If it were a chocolate bar it would have been called the *fun size*. There was nothing fun about it.

"And you've stopped seeing your counsellor now?"

"My psychiatrist. Yeah. I wanted it to be a new start coming here. I wanted to break away from that."

I didn't want to be the Girl Who Was Seeing the Shrink.

Doctor Fisher turned to the computer and scrolled, tapped in some notes.

"She said I was ready." I felt the need to explain. "It was a shared decision."

"But you still can't sleep?"

"That's not...I mean it's not just down to..."

"That's okay." Her voice was calm, soothing.

The room was warm. I had to keep talking.

"I just want some more meds really. That's what I came for." *Meds.* It sounds so much better than *drugs.*

"I see you've tried a few different drugs. None of them helped?"

"Some of them a little maybe. Not enough."

"I'm willing to try you on Somniclone. Doesn't look like you've been on that one. But do think some more about whether you might benefit from someone to talk to. If you don't want to see a psychiatrist right now, I could put you in touch with a counsellor."

Right now. Like it was inevitably going to happen someday. Like I was definitely going to need to...go through that again.

"Uh huh," I said. Play the game. Go along with it. Show willing. "Sure. Maybe. Is there a waiting list?" I hoped there was. I wanted a break from all of that. I wanted it so badly.

"Actually, no. We have a great team here at the university. I can get you started as soon as you're settled in."

I couldn't bear going straight back into it.

"Can I try the meds first? I'll get in touch as soon as I have my timetables set up and, sure, yeah I'll talk to someone." I was looking at my hands, picking at the skin around my nails. It's a habit I seem to have picked up. "If you think I should."

The doctor nodded and put her hand out, onto mine. She meant it to be comforting and reassuring, I know, but I withdrew instinctively.

"I'm here whenever you need to come and see me." She said it so calmly, so softly. Like she was talking to a stray dog, trying to comfort it.

"Yeah," I said again. I wanted to get the prescription and get out of there. I looked at where my watch would be if I was wearing one. I wished that I was. It's a good ruse, pretending you have to be somewhere. "You must be busy. I've taken up enough of your time."

She pulled her hand back and started to tap at the keyboard.

"Of course. It must be...I can't imagine how you...I'll print this off for you and, well, let me know how you get on with them."

I almost snatched the sheet from her hand. I was on my feet and heading for the door as soon as she gave it to me.

"Take care, Becky," she called after me, as I left. Without looking around, I waved my hand, still grasping my prescription.

Chapter Three

I manage to get through the Creative Non-Fiction lecture without crashing, but there are a few close calls. I drop my bag at the doorway, somehow it just slips from my grasp. As I bend down to pick it up, the kid behind me keeps walking, doesn't see that I stopped because he's too busy scrolling on his phone, almost falls on his face tripping over me.

"Shit. I'm sorry," I say.

He gives me this glare, like I did it on purpose or something.

I hike my bag onto my shoulder, so I don't cause any more accidents.

"What's with you?" Cally says, as we shuffle back to South.

"Huh?" I know what she's talking about, obviously. I don't really want to discuss it with her. I don't want to be the Girl Who Can't Sleep. I don't want to be...I don't want anyone here to start talking about what happened. I moved three hundred miles from home to get away from all that. I could have just gone to Harborough Uni. Some of my friends, well, some of the people I knew at college, not really friends, not friends at all...they went there. I would have known people. That would mean that they would have known me.

Being here is an escape.

"Dark rings. Falling asleep in the lecture. Clumsy." She pauses, but I know there's more coming. "Moody."

"I guess we don't know each other that well yet, Cal."

She does this little quick step around me, standing in my path, stopping me dead in my track.

"Hold up," she says. I kind of have to or I'll be walking over her. She grips my wrists, pulls me off to the side of the track. We sit on a wooden plank bench as students mill past us, going back to their dorms one way, going out to the SU the other.

I don't fight against her. I acquiesce. Here we go again, another opportunity to tell the story.

"Yeah. I don't sleep too well," I say, not looking at her.

"I've heard you bumbling around the flat at stupid o'clock. I figured."

Her room is next door to mine, no matter how quiet I have tried to be, I guess I wasn't quiet enough.

"Yeah," I say again.

"So…" She looks at me, even though I'm not looking at her, I can feel her eyes on me. I'm used to it, this feeling. Being observed. Being watched.

"I've been like this for a few years. Something happened…" I turn to look at her now, and see her eyebrows raise at this. "I don't really want to talk about it. I…I just didn't cope with it very well. Stopped eating, stopped sleeping. The eating thing…that was easier to deal with. Not easy, but easier. But still, I can't sleep."

"Not at all?"

"Brief little flashes of sleep. Just enough to keep me going, I guess. And micro-sleeps like in class just then. Mostly no one notices. Mostly people aren't watching out for me, I guess." I give her a little smile, try to show her that I appreciate her caring.

She's silent for a few moments. There's a look of concentration on her face.

"Is there anything I can do?" she asks, eventually.

I give her a big smile this time. "Just be you," I say. "Just be my mate."

"We don't know each other that well, you're right. But…I'm here for you. None of us know each other well here yet. Uni is scary enough without having to deal with all this crap you have to…okay?"

I nod, and I'm wondering whether to reach over and give her a hug when she puts her arm out for a fist bump. That will do.

We head back to the flat. My phone starts buzzing in my pocket as we start up the stairs. I let it ring off, and around twenty seconds later there's a sharp triple buzz that lets me know I have voicemail. I don't take it out to look as we are just getting to the door, and Cally's fishing around for her key.

"Fuck, why do I do this?" She's muttering under her breath as she roots through the contents of her backpack.

"I'll get it." My key is in the front pocket of my bag. I always keep it there when it's not next to my bed. I get it out and unlock the door.

"Cheers," she says. I let her in first and follow close behind.

Cally flops onto one of the large sofas and I settle into the other. The thing about never sleeping, one of the things about never sleeping, is that I am constantly exhausted. I feel like my body is on the edge of a precipice, like I'm constantly teetering on the brink. Trapped in some sort of in-between state. You know that feeling you get when you're just about to fall asleep and your mind starts to wander. Like it's flickering. An old television set switching between static and fragments of some crazy show like the Twilight Zone or something. All these pieces that don't make sense. Half the time I feel like that. The other half I have that groggy cotton-wool-head fuzz that you get when you're just waking up. That disorientation of the senses, the disjointed bleary buzz. Right now, it's that. That's how I feel. Cally is chatting to me and I can only half-concentrate on what she's saying. Half concentrating is more than I manage some days though.

She's kicked off her shoes and she's lying across the sofa now.

"Did you want to talk about what happened?" she asks. It must still be on her mind, I guess.

"Not really," I say.

Not at all.

Not ever.

I understand her curiosity. Most people start to ask questions when they feel comfortable enough with me. I try not to let people get too comfortable.

"I don't like to," I say. I hope that's enough.

"If you ever want to talk. You know where I am."

"Sure. Thanks."

It's unlikely that I will ever want to talk

about it. My parents paid good money for me to have someone to talk to about it, and it took over a year of sessions to even start. I never told her everything, the psychiatrist. I never told her much at all. I've not told anyone exactly what happened. Not so far. I have given versions of the story, but only the parts that I can bear to talk about at the time.

Cally holds her phone above her and scrolls and taps through her social media. She doesn't ask any more questions, and I am relieved.

We share the flat with Eamon and Heidi, who live in the rooms to the other side of the kitchen area. I guess I'm closer to Cally because of our shared classes, but also there's a kind of sisterhood with us being next-door-neighbours. Cally is from Liverpool, so we are also the Northern contingent here in the flat. Eamon comes from London, and Heidi from some small town near Brighton. I can't remember its name. Despite the fact we were randomly thrown together into the flat, we do get on alright. So far. None of us is dirty or untidy or inconsiderate, so that's a good start.

When I look across again, Cally's phone is lying on her chest, and she's asleep. I have a sharp pang of jealousy, just for a moment. It's so easy for some people. If you've always been able to sleep anytime, anywhere, you will have taken it for granted. If it's ever taken away from you, that ability, you'll miss it. Appreciate it while you can.

When I finally get into my room and empty my pockets out to get ready for bed, I see my phone screen and remember the call I missed. It was from my mum. The clock tells me it's half-past eleven, just gone. I could leave it until tomorrow, but when I do that she gets upset. She knows I'm awake all night. She knows I will have seen her missed call. She worries about me. A lot. It's understandable considering what happened. I have to phone her back. Tonight.

I get changed first. Even though I can't sleep, I go through the motions. It's one of the few things I learned from my psychiatrist.

"Don't go to bed with the mindset that you won't be able to sleep," she told me. "Always go through your night-time routine, just as you would have done...before." She always sounded nervous or uncertain or afraid of talking about the *before*. Or the *triggering event*. I found that fascinating, considering she was the professional.

Another hot tip she gave me was: "If you can't sleep, just lie still. Be motionless. Give your body the opportunity to do as little as possible. Let it rest."

So that's what I do. I have built myself a routine. Not the routine that I had *before*, because I'm going to be honest with you here, I never had a routine before. I was sixteen. I had no reason to have a routine. I just did what I wanted. I always did what I wanted.

My routine comprises all the usual things. I go into the little bathroom that Cally and I share, and I remove my make-up. I moisturise, clean my teeth, brush my hair. If I don't plan on washing it the next day, I tug it back in a ponytail. I wear a T-shirt and sweats in bed in winter, shorts or pants in summer. I don't own pyjamas. I definitely don't own a onesie. Telling you about it, describing it to you like this, it's therapeutic for me. It's like a pattern, a rhythm. These are the things I need. I hope that if I keep doing this, if I repeat the rhythms that eventually the next part of the song will drop in: sleep.

I'm aware that I'm fulfilling all the actions of my routine tonight before I phone my mother. I'm putting it off, procrastinating, but once I'm clean and dressed in my nightwear, there's no more stalling.

I've not listened to the voicemail. I just swipe my

phone open and click the button to make the call. It's almost midnight. I should feel bad about leaving it so late. I feel resentful that I have to interrupt my routine to call her at all.

She picks up on the third ring.

"Rebecca, sweetheart."

I imagine her spending the whole evening sitting with her phone, waiting for me to return the call, and I almost feel bad.

"Mum. Hi. Were you in bed? Sorry to call so late."

I can hear Dad in the background. She must be in bed already. They must be.

"It's fine, love." She shushes Dad and speaks to me in hushed tones.

"I haven't heard from you. I was worried."

We spoke about a week ago. Maybe it was longer. I sometimes lose track of time. My meds and my condition: both of them together conspire against me.

"Sorry," I say. "I'm fine though."

I'm not fine. I'm never fine. I doubt I will ever be fine again. Not after, well, you know.

"Can you remember to call me more often, please?"

One of the reasons that I *don't* call more often is that most of our conversations are like this.

No real content. Nothing said between us. We don't know how to talk to each other anymore. Not with everything that has happened.

"Okay, Mum. I promise I will."

She doesn't ask whether I'm sleeping yet. She doesn't ask if I've got myself a shrink here. She doesn't ask about medications or treatments or anything like that. These omissions mean a lot to me. I'm grateful.

"Are you enjoying your classes?" she asks.

"Yeah. They're fine." We have had this conversation before too.

"That's good. Just do your best, love. That's all we want. Just the best for you."

"Okay, Mum."

There's a silence on the line, and then Mum says, "Goodnight then, love. I love you."

"Yeah," I say. "You too. Goodnight."

I click the end call button before she can think of anything else to say, then I lie in the darkness, awake and alone.

Chapter Four

Sometimes I close my eyes. Sometimes I don't bother. The darkness looks the same either way. My mind swims with thoughts. My mother. My brother. My stupid fucked-up brain. I wonder whether I'll ever sleep properly again. This is not what my psychiatrist taught me.

Be still. When thoughts come, let them float away. Be calm...

My thoughts do not float. They are the anchors that weigh me down. I sink into a deep gloom that I'm reluctant to call depression because I don't need any more labels.

This all started immediately after what happened to Jordan. It wasn't a slow creep of sleeplessness, it hit me all at once. I was completely unprepared for it. I went from being a typical lie-in-bed-until-midday-at-weekend teenager to a walking zombie. I wasn't exactly a try-hard at school before, but I coasted along just fine, thank you very much. The insomnia began as I was coming to the end of my exams. I'd already crammed in a *lot* of revision, mostly thanks to Jordan. He pushed me a lot harder than my parents ever have. Probably because he *could*, you know. Coming from Mum and Dad, I think it would have felt like pressure. Coming from Jordan, it always felt like gentle encouragement. He is the reason that I am here now, despite everything. This course was his dream, this is the career path he would have chosen, if choices hadn't been taken from him.

I stumbled through my A-Levels, but without Jordan there to encourage me, I had to find the strength and stamina within myself to succeed. My brain is a constant obstacle in my desire to make it. I forget things so easily now. Concentration is sometimes impossible to maintain. I am running on empty, but I'm still running. I can't give up. I owe it to Jordan, to his memory, to succeed.

It's hard to describe to someone who hasn't experienced insomnia quite how terrible it can feel, and how debilitating it can be. Lying here in the night, every night, it's a lonely, liminal existence.

A darkened room is never completely dark. There are always points where the light finds its way in. Not just the edges of the curtains, but between the weave of the cotton. Beneath the door. It always finds a way.

My eyes are accustomed to it now, this blackness. I'm sure my night vision has improved through months of lying awake in the near-dark. I'm sure my brain has become accustomed to seeing the dark side of life too.

I see a movement. Or I sense a movement, I'm not sure which. Either way, I know something moved. By the door, in the corner. I'm sure of it. I'm almost sure of it. I keep my eyes open, focussing on a spot just off to the side of where I saw it. Looking directly at it will mean not seeing it. I don't know the science behind that, but I know from experience that it is true.

I look, and I look, and the more I concentrate, the more I am sure that there is someone in my room.

I keep perfectly still. I would stop breathing if I could. I make my breaths as shallow as possible.

Think. Think.

The first thing I think is that there's no point trying to hide. If there is someone in my room, what am I going to do? Lie in bed until morning, trying not to breathe? And then what? It will start to become light, and I'll be lying here looking at somebody who will be standing there looking at me. The idea of it becomes comical in my mind. A bizarre standoff. The two of us in an awkward staring contest, neither sure what to do next.

If there's someone there, and they want to hurt me, it's too late really to hide. They know I am here. I think I know that they are there, but the more I think about it, the less it makes sense. I relax my breathing, stop making the effort to conceal myself. Just to be sure though, I'm going to have to get up.

I sketch a quick plan in my mind. I'll throw off the covers, run over and ambush them. Slam into their gut, try to wind them. The unexpected is usually the best way. The element of surprise and all that.

I try to wriggle my knees up surreptitiously. I push my hands down onto the bed and spring up, charging into the corner like an American footballer. I collide with something firm; it feels like my legs are being grabbed. I panic, thrash,

and realise that I've become tangled in the straps of my rucksack. I thrust my palm against the light switch, and the harsh light reveals the truth.

I'm fighting with my jacket and bag.

For fuck's sake.

My jacket hangs on a peg, high enough on the wall to make it look to my addled, sleep-deprived mind that it's a person. The bulk of my bag beneath it completes the illusion.

"Well done, idiot," I mutter to myself, and gently punch my coat.

I hear footsteps in the corridor outside, and then there's a sharp tapping at my door.

In a hushed voice, outside: "Becky? You okay?" It's Cally. How do I start to explain to her that I was having an altercation with my clothing?

She's wearing a white fluffy onesie with a hood that's designed to make her look like a unicorn, the horn a mix of pastel rainbow shades. Her hood is down, but she still looks ridiculous. I think for a flash that if there was something going on in my room it would have been quite something to see a face-off between this fluffy character and a potentially savage assailant. A few minutes ago, I was fearing for my life in the face of a jacket and bag combo. Now I'm standing at my door talking to a unicorn.

"Did I wake you up? I'm so sorry."

I'm starting to feel glad that I told her about my sleeping issues. It makes this a little easier.

"I heard a noise. Like, I don't know, clattering? Crashing? I don't know what it was. What happened?"

She casts her eye over me. I must look reasonably normal because she doesn't pass comment.

"I was just getting something out of my bag, and I dropped it. It's pretty heavy." I roll my eyes in feigned astonishment at my own stupidity.

"That's the second time you've dropped it. Nothing breakable in there, I hope?"

"I took my laptop out when I came in here." I gesture at the table, as if to confirm the words. "Nothing else, no. Books. Pencil case. Usual stuff."

She looks at her watch.

"You haven't slept yet?"

I shake my head. "Maybe five minutes. Ten. I drop off for a few minutes and then, I don't know, my body realises it's doing it and, next thing I know, I'm awake again."

"It's six o'clock, almost. I don't think I'll be able to get back to sleep now."

I frown and look at the ground.

"Hey, it's okay. I'm a light sleeper," she says. "At least I *can* sleep, eh?"

It's so good of her to make light of this. I appreciate it so much.

She looks at me for a moment and says, "Want to go get breakfast? The café opens at six. It'll be open by the time we get there. If it's not too early for you?"

Because my body clock is screwed, I can pretty much eat at any time of the day. When this started, I used to eat at every time of the day. I mean that was, in part, related to what happened. Coping mechanisms. Involuntary psychological and physiological responses, whatever.

"That sounds good," I smile. "Let me get some proper clothes on and I'll knock for you when I'm ready."

"Okay. Five minutes. Come get me. You're sure you're okay?"

I smile and nod and she pops back into her room.

I flop onto my bed, kick my legs in frustration, and let myself feel terribly stupid for a minute before I get up again and put on my clothes.

Quarter of an hour later, we are sitting across the table from each other in the café. *Rachel's Coffee House*, it's called. That seems like a lame attempt to make this sterile, generic cafeteria into something more attractive to students.

Despite the time, and the fact that *Rachel's* has only just opened, we aren't the only people here. There's a couple, or at least a boy and a girl who are leaning towards each other at a table in the corner. I don't know them, but there's over ten thousand students on campus, and I'm less than a month into living here. Bang in the centre of the room are a group of seven girls, kitted out in jogging gear, sports leggings, hi vis vests. They are chatting animatedly. If I had just woken up, they'd be too much for me. There's a girl at the till in front of us that I'm sure I recognise from somewhere, but I can't place her. She's probably in one of my lecture groups. There are about sixty people in the shared class with Cally's group. It's a closed community on campus, but it's still a large one.

I order pancakes and bacon, and Cally wrinkles her nose.

"I thought you'd be a full English girl like me," she says. "Being Northern and that."

"We're more cosmopolitan in Harborough, clearly," I smile. "My brother went on holiday to the States a few years back and came back with this fetish for pancakes."

"You didn't get to go?"

I pause. Images flash through my mind. I push them away.

"No," I say, brusquely. I flick my eyes away, compose myself.

She gets her coffee and we sit at a table by

the window.

I can see down the path into Main from here. There are the beginnings of some activity now, even at this time.

A few random people, wandering around, wrapped up against the late Autumn chill. Despite being awake at all hours, I tend to not bother being out and about at this time of the day. Nothing much happens.

"Hey," Cally says, nudging my arm. I've been staring out of the window, ignoring her.

"Sorry," I say.

"Thought you were drifting off there." She takes a sip of her coffee. "Way too hot. Yeuch."

"I...get distracted easily. My concentration is shit. The..." I almost say the meds, but I don't want to talk about that. I don't want her thinking I'm doped up. I'd love her to think that I'm just a normal person. I mean, I am. I can't sleep. That's all it is. "The insomnia," I say.

"Your brain must be exhausted," she says, trying to make sense of me. "Being switched on all the time."

"Must be."

She picks at her food, but I can see her mind isn't on it. She's as distracted as I am.

"Can I ask you something?" she says.

Here we go. What will it be?

"You can ask," I say. "I might not want to answer though."

She smiles slightly. Not a proper smile, just a trace.

"What was it? What happened? What started all this?"

I told her yesterday that I didn't want to talk about it. I'm sure I told her.

She looks a little embarrassed and starts to cut into her egg instead of looking at me. She sticks the blade of her knife into the yolk and it bursts its contents over the plate. The thick viscous flood runs into her beans, starts to seep into the toast. I fixate on it. Then I speak.

"My brother was...my brother died."

She coughs a little on her mouthful of sausage and egg, and swallows too quickly.

"I'm sorry."

It's such a common response. *I'm sorry*. Like it was her fault. Like she caused it, or could somehow have prevented it. I didn't even know her then. She was living some other life, on the other side of the Pennines, at her own school, finishing her exams. *Happy.* I'm sure she was happy. She wasn't losing her brother; I know that much. I shrug and push my plate away. I've hardly eaten anything. The taste of maple syrup reminds me of Jordan.

Chapter Five

I didn't get to go to America with my parents and Jordan. Instead, I stayed with my grandma in Bridlington for a fortnight.

My dad was working out in the States, and the company gave him a ticket for Mum. We weren't a rich family. I mean we were comfortable, never short of money, but not rich. Not pay-for-two-kids-to-go-to-America rich. They promised that I could go the next time, that there would be a next time, but there never was.

I didn't often see my grandma. Bridlington is around an hour and a half from where we lived, where my parents still live. You know what it's like though, life happens, and you never quite get around to doing all the things you could. Or should. Grandma died that winter so, looking back, I'm glad I got to spend that time with her. Back then though, when I was there, I resented it. Not her. Just the fact that I was there and not in the States. Any kid would feel the same.

I had some crazy idea of what Fort Worth was like. That's where they were. Not one of the main tourist destinations, just some place in Texas that sounded like an offshoot of Dallas. Still, I imagined the bright-lights-big-city flashy immensity of the places I had seen on television.

Jordan told me he was bored most of the time. They were in the middle of nowhere, no internet, no other kids, nothing to do.

I wish I were at Grandma's with you, he told me. I thought he was playing it up for me, trying to make me feel better. He did that. He always did that.

I didn't get to play with any other kids either. Jordan and I shared our intercontinental isolation. I didn't mind though. I liked being alone. Back then I wasn't so concerned with fitting in. I hadn't grown to want the affirmation of others. I was happy being an individual, I didn't care what people thought. I do now.

Like I said, I hadn't seen much of Grandma Mary before, but we clicked quickly. She lived in a cottage on the hillside, overlooking the sea. It was like being in the crow's nest on a ship, looking out of the bedroom window when I woke every morning. And yes, I woke every morning then, because I slept every night. She was an early riser and once she was up and about, I couldn't sleep any longer.

She would pick up her walking stick and head off to the market by nine o'clock. If I didn't want to be left behind, I had to be up too. It was my only chance to get outside, that little slot in the mornings.

On my third day in the cottage, I overslept and found myself alone. I lay in bed a little while, but without phone signal I was at a loss for anything to do there. I had breakfast and pottered around aimlessly. When she still wasn't back by eleven, I had to try to amuse myself. I started to explore the rooms. I thought that I should stay out of Grandma's bedroom, but anywhere else was fair game.

In the living room was a heavy oak sideboard. I opened it up to reveal coasters, tablecloths, serving bowls, and a stack of board games. Cluedo, Monopoly, Chess, Scrabble. All the traditionals.

Grandma Mary had lived alone for four years since Grandad Pete passed away. I hate that phrase. *Passed away.* It's not as bad as *fell asleep,* but it's close. He died. If more people talked openly about death, if dying wasn't such a taboo subject, I might have found it easier to deal with what happened to Jordan. Easier. Not easy. It could never be easy. Anyway, she didn't have anyone to play those games with. I felt a thud in my chest like indigestion. I shut the cupboard back up, but that night I offered to play with her. She lit up at the suggestion, like I'd offered her something precious. I suppose I had. Time and companionship were all I had to give, but they were what Grandma craved the most.

One evening, in my second week there, we sat listening to one of her cassettes, playing Scrabble. I didn't know anyone else who owned a cassette player, never mind cassette tapes. It was like something from the distant past, a curio. There had been a label on the tape once, but it had rubbed off over the years. Now it was a plain cream colour, faded by time. It was a man singing; crooning, I think they call it. It was fine. Inoffensive. She liked it and that was enough for me. I didn't recognise the song, but Grandma hummed along. It seemed like an involuntary action, something inside her synchronized with the sound and she joined in.

We had already played one game, which she won, and were a few moves into the second. I was thinking about how she and Grandad must have sat here like this, playing this game together. Maybe they listened to the same song. Maybe he always let her win, and maybe he didn't have to. I was thinking about how you can be with someone for so long, and then they can just be gone.

"What's it like?" I asked her. I was fifteen. I didn't know much about anything. I didn't know about tact or subtlety. "Losing someone. Like Grandad?"

She looked up from the Scrabble board, and her tongue moved over her lips. I let her think of the right words to describe it. Despite how little I knew, I knew that thoughts like that took time.

She bent forwards and laid a word on the tiles.

E – M – blank – T – Y

It was the blank that hit me. Right there in the middle. That hole. You can make out what the word is, like you can almost make out what your life is, without the person you've lost. Still you know that there is something unspoken missing. An empty space.

I nodded. I thought I understood. I thought the image translated inside my head to something like the emotions that she felt, but I never understood the language of loss until I lost Jordan.

Grandma Mary was my mother's mother. I guess they grew apart like my mother and I, just not for the same reasons. When Mum came to pick me up, they hovered around each other in the living room, passing pleasantries and then sitting in an awkward silence while I gathered the rest of my belongings. Somewhere along the line they had forgotten how to communicate with each other. That bond had been broken. I wondered then if that would happen to Mum and me, although I suppose I always knew it would. We left with well wishes and bland pleasantries. I never saw my Grandma again.

My eyes snap open and I'm in the café. Cally is sitting opposite me still, reading something on her phone.

"Shit!" I say. "Was I asleep?"

"Not for long. I expected you to be out longer. Ten minutes, tops."

My pancakes are cold, and Cally's plate is clean.

"Was it good? I'm sorry for…"

"It's fine," she says. "I understand. Well, I don't actually understand, but I get that this just happens to you. I won't take it personally."

I give her a smile.

"One minute you were talking to me, the next you looked down onto your plate and whoosh you were gone. Does it always happen like that?"

"Well, I've never seen what I do but I've been told before that I do this. That this is how it usually goes. I'm never out for long though."

"Should I wake you when it happens, or what? What's best?" She sounds genuinely concerned about me.

"Oh fuck, no. Don't wake me. Those little snoozes are the only sleeps I get. I doubt that I could survive without them. If you sit patiently for ten minutes, I'll be back with you."

She nods and drinks the last of her coffee.

"Before you dropped off...I asked you about what happened. You said that your brother had died. I didn't...I didn't know what to say, to be honest. I have a sister, and I can't imagine how it would be. Really, it must be awful for you. Were you close?"

My mouth feels parched, desiccated. I breathe in and then exhale the word "yes".

She nods silently.

I don't usually talk about Jordan. I don't want to.

"He was the best. The best big brother you could imagine. He always thought of me. Always put me first. He was my parents' favourite. He was a boy. He was born first. But...he made up for that by treating me like a princess." That's more than I have said about him in months. "I loved him so much. I love him. I still love him."

"Oh, Becky." She reaches over to me and I let her put her hand on mine. There's a lull while she thinks of what to say next.

"The insomnia began straight after he…straight after what happened?"

"Yes. When he died. From that day on. I've not had a full night's sleep." I don't want to tell her about the psychiatrist, dear Doctor Balliol, or about all the different drugs that I've been on and off. Right now, I have her sympathy. I don't want her judgement.

"I feel like I've brought your day down already," I say.

"No, no. It's fine. It's been nice being up early, eating a good breakfast. Sorry you didn't get your food while it was hot. We should do it again sometime. If you have another morning where you're lying awake and alone, just knock for me."

She's so sweet. Really. Her accent is all sharp and spiky, but her personality is like her unicorn onesie. Soft and fluffy. I hope we are going to be friends. I feel like we might be already.

"I will do," I say. And I mean it.

Chapter Six

University life so far has been a constant shift from lectures to laziness. I'm trying my best to do everything that everyone else does. I'm lucky to have a group of flatmates that are easy to get along with. It makes it less of an effort for me to socialise. And it is an effort. I'm naturally introverted. As a kid I always had Jordan as a constant companion. I didn't need anyone else but him. In my teens I wasn't really that successful in making and keeping friends. I'm partly to blame, of course. I didn't want to put myself out there. Also, I just didn't enjoy the cliques, the bitching and general competitiveness of the girls I knew.

In my second year of high school I fell into a friendship with another shy, quiet girl called Mischa Brake. I guess we were both the same, so the two of us tumbled together. I didn't set out to befriend her, I wasn't looking for a companion. Still, it happened. She understood the difficulties of making friends, and she liked the things I liked. We ran our own two-person book club. We had sleepovers at each other's homes. We danced around her parents' kitchen to her mum's old Rolling Stones records. My folks didn't have anything like that. Music didn't exist at our place until Jordan started listening to a band called The Testaments. (They're an indie rock band from near Harborough, if you haven't heard of them. Check them out.) Anyway, Jordan was really into this band, and hearing their music through the wall that divided our rooms was enough to get me into them too. I'm getting side-tracked. I do that.

Anyway, one morning I went to Mischa's house as I had every other morning, to walk to school with her. It was raining, and I was soaked by the time I got there. I expected she would invite me in, let me dry my hair. When it was cold or wet, her mum usually stepped up to offer us a lift, so when she answered the door, I was hopeful. Instead of inviting me in, she stood in the entrance, leaving me in the street, in the rain.

"I'm going to be taking Mischa to school from now on," she said.

I misunderstood at first. I thought she had meant that she was going to drive both of us. She stood, staring at me with an expression of distaste that I had never seen before. I didn't know what to say. I didn't understand.

Mischa and I had been friends, best friends, for two years by this point. Her mother had played games with us, helped me with homework, taught me how to make triple chocolate brownies. Her mother did the things with me that I wished my own mother would do. We were close. I had felt like part of their family. After all that, she looked at me that morning as though I was dirt.

"Don't come around here anymore," she said.

"I'm sorry, what?"

That's when it hit me.

She meant it. Something had changed. Something awful had happened.

"And please, don't speak to Mischa at school. I don't want this to become any more difficult for her than it already is."

Difficult for Mischa? I stood, open-mouthed, not comprehending. I tried to look past Mrs. Brake, looking for Mischa. If I could get her attention, work out what was happening, perhaps I could make everything right.

She was nowhere to be seen.

Her mother looked at me, one last time, and closed the door in my face.

I stood there on the doorstep. The rain mingled with my tears, washed over me. I was cold. I was lost. Nothing made sense. The world was a grey place.

It didn't take long for me to work things out. When I got to school there was a note tucked into my locker.

One word. Scrawled in marker pen on a scrap of paper.

Dyke.

I didn't even know what the word meant.

I looked around me. I felt like an antelope on the plains, in open sight, feeling the eyes of a hunter burning into them. It wasn't just one hunter though; it was a pack. Everyone was against me. I was on my own.

As the day progressed, I heard whispers as I passed by other students. They would see me coming and turn away, retreating into their groups.

I once heard someone say that the only thing worse than being talked about is not being talked about. It's so untrue. Being talked about, having rumours spread about you, being the subject of everyone's conversations, being the headline in the gossip groups, it's unbearable.

Like I said, I never had lots of friends, and I was happy that way. I never wanted to stand out. That day, everything changed. I became a focus point. Everyone's attention, everyone's negativity, it was all directed at me. I wanted to curl up into a ball, become small and invisible. I lost Mischa, and I lost my anonymity. That day, I wasn't sure which I missed the most.

When I got home from school, I shut myself in my room. I was finally alone. I could get into my bed, hide under the covers, shut out everything and everybody. All I wanted was to pretend that the outside world did not exist, because it wasn't a place I wanted to be. Everyone sucked. Everything sucked. Fuck it all.

When my mum came to knock for me at dinner time, I said nothing. I buried my head under my pillow, and I cried until my eyes ran dry. She brought food to my room and tried to talk to me, but I didn't know what to say. I couldn't repeat that word to her. The word on the paper. *Dyke*. Was that what I was? I didn't even know, then. I didn't know who I was or what I wanted. I hadn't even thought about it. I was just Becky Braithwaite. I was just me. I certainly wasn't ready to have that conversation with my mum. I guess Mum thought I was having some kind of teenage drama. She hated anything like that. Didn't know how to deal with it. I was glad. It meant she stayed away, left me to brew.

Jordan came in around ten and ran straight up to my room. He had been out with his girlfriend

Jennie, a mousy girl that he'd met in a coffee shop in town. She was nice enough, I suppose. I didn't really know her. That night though, I knew that I wished he was at home with me, not out somewhere with her. I needed him. He was the only one I could talk to.

Anyway, Jordan knocked on my door and I knew it was him before I heard his voice. He had this certain way of knocking. Firm, friendly. I can't really describe it. I would always know. I'll never hear that knock again. I can't tell you how much that sucks.

I unlocked my door and we stood there for a couple of seconds looking at each other. His stance went from relaxed, calm, and happy to edgy and concerned in a snap.

"What happened?" he said.

I threw myself into his arms, and he held me. I sobbed against his chest, and he held me. I told him what had happened, and he held me.

"It doesn't matter what other people think," he said. "It doesn't matter what they say."

But it did matter. It mattered more than anything. It mattered because it had cost me my best friend. It had cost me what little confidence I had. It had made me the centre of attention and I hated it.

We sat on my bed and he stroked my hair. I loved it when he did that. It felt so soothing. Something about the way he did it...I don't know, it just made me feel cared for. Cared about. It's those little things...I miss him so much.

I tried though. I tried not to care what other people said or thought about me. I heard Jordan's voice in my head every time. When I heard them talking about me, I didn't turn the other way and take a different route. I would stand there, almost daring them to carry on.

It made people uncomfortable.

I liked that.

Rather than make people stop talking about me, not reacting as they expected had the effect of making them change what they were saying.

Instead of being a *pussyeater bushmuncher lesbo queer* I became *freaky weirdo creepy*.

Was I any of those things?

Was I all of them?

I was trying to work out for myself who or what I was. The last thing I needed was that kind of pressure.

I completely isolated myself, unintentionally, by being an introvert, and then intentionally by failing to conform.

I had Jordan, and that was all that mattered.

Chapter Seven

Between lectures, I grab a sandwich in *Rachel's* and get my laptop out of my rucksack. If they ran a loyalty card I'd be quids in here. I'm not a lazy chef, but I'm a lazy girl. I can't be bothered walking back over to South and making lunch when *Rachel's* is so convenient. I have an hour between Digital Publishing and Cultural Creativity modules. I'm not wasting it on walking.

It's always busy here at lunchtime, but not so busy that I can't get a table. There's quite a shift in the atmosphere between the early morning crowd that were here at six o'clock and the more talkative, upbeat customers that are here now. The energy feels different. If I'm honest, I prefer the feel of early morning. It's gentler, more laid back.

I pick at my sandwich and stare at my screen, waiting for inspiration to strike. Looking at the blank screen when I've just started writing something is the worst part for me. If I had a few words down, others would follow. I could hang other sentences from them like a tub of Tumblin' Monkeys. My brain is as blank as the page. I type:

Week Three

I can't hang many monkeys off that.

I sit back, drink some of my Coke and let out a frustrated sigh. If I slept more maybe I'd be able to think of more creative ideas. Maybe not though. Maybe it's just a convenient excuse.

Week Three. That's all I have. I let my eyes wander, distracted. That's when I first notice her.

I don't know whether I caught sight of her in my peripheral vision, or if my sixth sense kicked in. Sometimes you can just feel it, can't you? When someone is looking at you. I had this sensation, a tingling, that made me turn my head to the right.

A brown-haired girl, chatting with what I assumed from the back of the head was a boy. I shouldn't assume. Shaved heads seem to be the style for girls too, at this university anyway. It's an expression of personality, isn't it? I guess that's why my hair is such a mess. It reflects my life, my personality. Blonde, unruly, uncared for.

I realise I'm staring now, while my actions catch up with my brain. Staring at the shaved head. The girl has turned her gaze away. She *was* looking at me though, directly at me. I flash my eyes back to my laptop, try to get on with my work. I have to write a short report once a week. It helps to build my portfolio. *Formative*, the lecturer calls it.

Basically, it's work that we do that we don't get marked on; it doesn't count towards our degree. It's practice, an opportunity to write. Some of the others resent spending the time on pieces that aren't directly assessed. Fuck, I just want to write. I want to improve on what I do; I want to learn new things. Besides, I have so much time to spare, I may as well use it productively.

I tap in a few words, but I'm still distracted. I don't really know what I'm writing. I can feel the weight of her stare on me again. I try to look without turning my head this time; I move my eyes slightly, tilt them back down. It would be handy right now to be one of those animals that has excellent peripheral vision. Not *eyes like a hawk*, that just means that you can see at a distance, pick out detail. The animals with the best peripheral vision are the hunted, not the hunters. You know those cute memes you see of derpy looking goats? Their eyes look like little dots right on the sides of their faces...that's so they can see all around them when their heads are down, grazing. They can go on with all their essential daily routines and still look out for danger. That's what I need right now. Eyes like a goat. I wouldn't have to turn my head to see what I know is true: she's staring. Staring. Staring.

I've felt this before. When I was at school. Everybody's eyes on me. Singled out. Observed. Watched. Mocked. I take a breath and turn my head to look back at her. Again, as soon as I look, she looks away.

I feel a knot in my throat. Taking a gulp of my Coke doesn't help. I can just about see my reflection in the laptop screen. I wonder if I have something on my face, or if my hair is sticking up, or maybe I've wiped mascara over myself. I do these things sometimes. Maybe there's a reason she keeps looking. I don't know her. I don't recognise her. I look back again, just to check.

She sees me, says something to her companion, and gets to her feet.

She's coming over.

I look down at my screen, focus on my words. I'm wearing earphones so I can pretend I don't hear her. I can make her think I don't see her.

There's no hiding though. She's in front of me now. She waves a hand in my line of vision.

I pull out my earphones.

"Hi," she says.

She doesn't sound angry or unkind.

"Hello." I'm tentative, but I reply.

"You're Becky?"

I frown. She knows me from somewhere

then. I'm sure I've never seen her before.

"You don't remember me, do you? Me and Lee met you Fresher's week." She laughs. "You must have been drunk!"

I smile. "Must have been." I never drink. Not now. I genuinely don't remember her though.

"Want to come and sit with us? I was trying to get your attention, but you're all caught up in your music and…" She looks over at my screen. "Coursework, I guess."

"Yeah, we have so much to do." I say it in a way that I hope tells her that I'm not interested in joining them.

She nods. "You have to take a break sometime."

I keep that tiny smile on my face and don't say any more.

"Okay," she says, when I've made her feel uncomfortable enough. "Nice to see you anyway. Come over when you're done if you fancy a chat."

"Thanks," I say. "I will." I won't. "It's good to see you too." I'm indifferent. I really don't care. I didn't want to be interrupted, even though I'm achieving next to nothing. I didn't want company.

She goes back to her seat and speaks a few words to Lee. Of course, I can't hear, but Lee turns around and looks at me.

She probably told her (because yes, the shaven-headed person is a girl) that I'm a bitch.

Whatever. I keep reminding myself that I want to fit in, but it's so hard when I don't want to talk to anyone. My lack of sleep leaves me so tetchy that I can't even bear to be around myself sometimes.

Unease, uncertainty and paranoia are not the monsters that hide under the bed. They are not lurking in the darkness. They are portable. You can put them in your pocket and carry them with you for the whole day. Lying awake in a semi-dark room at three in the morning, or sitting in a crowded cafeteria at noon, those feelings can strike anywhere. I don't want to be watched. I don't even want to be seen.

Chapter Eight

Weekend. Heidi's joined the rowing team, so she was up and away at six this morning. I didn't see her, but I heard the distant sounds from the kitchen that confirmed that she was up and about. It's comforting, somehow, knowing that there are other people around. I didn't drag myself out of bed to join Heidi for coffee, but knowing that I *could* if I wanted to gives me a sense that I'm not completely alone. Night-time can feel like a cocoon. Like I'm sealed up in a chrysalis, waiting for daytime, for the right time to emerge, and spread my wings.

Eamon is off to watch a football match. He invited the three of us to join him, but with Heidi already having other plans it seemed easy for Cally and I to make our excuses. *Another time*, we said. Maybe I meant it. I've never been to a game. Jordan wasn't into football. I suppose because my dad isn't. Never watched it on television, nothing. Jordan's thing was music. He took guitar lessons at school, and got pretty good. He tried to teach me, more than once. I kept complaining about it hurting my fingers. He said I'd get used to it, that my fingers would get harder. That was meant to make me feel better, but it had the opposite effect. I didn't want my fingers to be hard. I imagined calluses, the dry hard skin that Mum got on her feet in the summer when she'd been wearing sandals without socks for weeks. So, I never learned. I wish I had. I wish I had let him teach me, that he had passed on that part of himself to me. After…when Jordan…after what happened, I wanted to keep his guitar, but Mum wanted to get rid of it. She couldn't bear to have it in the house, she said. I wanted it so badly. I prickle with resentment even thinking about it.

Really, I wanted to learn piano. I had visions of Jordan on guitar, me on keyboards, playing in some club somewhere. People knowing who we were; it excited me, and it terrified me. Being seen means being judged. It always means that. I wanted to be just well known enough to have a small group of followers who loved us, rather than being in the critical eye of the masses. But when I asked my parents, they said it was too expensive. They couldn't afford a piano. They couldn't afford lessons. No matter how many times I asked, how hard I begged. I said I'd get a part-time job, that I'd pay them back, but the answer was always *no*.

So I'd sit in Jordan's room while he practiced playing guitar, and wish that one day I could create something, that I could do something, that one day I could be more than the little sister.

With Eamon and Heidi out for the day, I listen for the sound of Cally waking up and shuffling around her room. I'm pretty tuned in to her movements. I hear her walk across the room, open her wardrobe, rattle through the hangers. There's a lull while she pulls on her clothes, and then the click-open of her door. She usually goes straight to the bathroom, takes a pee, washes, cleans her teeth, all that boring daily routine. She's pretty quick though, I never have to wait long to use our shared toilet if I need it. One thing about Cally, she always wears make-up, even if she's only staying in the flat. I sometimes rub on some foundation if I'm a bit spotty but, on the whole, I try to rock the hot mess look. I'm joking; I accept I'm a mess.

I give it ten minutes after I hear her flush the toilet and toddle around to the lounge, and then I make my own way through. She's brought the duvet from her room and she's curled on one of the sofas watching a hospital drama on Netflix. It's Chase MD, this trashy TV show about a doctor who's even more messed up than his patients. His patients are even more messed up than I am. It's simple escapism; one of those programmes you don't have to think about too much to be able to enjoy. That's lucky because thinking is not my strong point.

"Morning." I beam a smile at her, and she returns it.

"Alright," she says in her broad Scouse accent.

She has coffee already; I make some for myself and settle onto the other sofa. Weekends are for being lazy.

"Are you regretting not going to the football?" she laughs.

"Fuck no. Coffee and *Chase MD* with you...couldn't think of anything I'd rather be doing."

We both laugh at that. It's so good to be able to relax with someone again, to be able to chat and giggle and feel like I can be myself. To feel like I don't have to worry about people talking about me. To be away from home. My past. Everything.

My phone starts to ring on the arm of the sofa next to me, I jump slightly.

"Sorry," I say to Cally, and click the green icon to answer.

"Hello?"

At the other end of the line I can hear

background noise. It sounds busy. People chatting, street bustle. Breathing, but no words.

"Hello?" I repeat. I look over at Cally and shrug.

Still nothing. Non-silent silence.

Is it ever really silent? In the quiet of night, I find myself aware of every little noise. My ears pick up all the subtle sounds: static, white noise, heartbeat thud.

One last time: "Hello?"

When there's still no response, I click *end call*.

"What's that?" Cally says.

"No one there. Probably some auto dial trying to sell me something." I look at the screen before I put it down. Unknown Number. Of course. I expected nothing else.

"I never give my number to anyone since I got my new phone. Once they get your details they don't give up, do they?" She slurps her coffee and turns back to the television.

We watch in comfortable silence until the end of the show. Before it runs on to the next episode, she nudges me with her foot to get my attention.

"Hey, you going to come out tonight? We're thinking of hitting the SU bar. Nothing heavy."

We've been out a bunch of times since we arrived. She knows I don't drink. It's nice to still be included though.

"Sure, I say. Just us and the other two?"

"Yeah to start with. I'm sure there will be other people we know in the bar though."

I guess she interpreted my question to infer that I wanted a larger group. I'd be happy if we were the only people in the bar though. We won't be.

"Okay. Can we get there early and get somewhere to sit? I don't want to be on my feet all night."

There are lots of tables in the bar, but there are lots more students than there are tables. We've turned up late a couple of times and had to stand in dark corners hovering all night with drinks in hand, people shoving past us, into us, around us.

She must remember the last time too. She smiles and agrees.

"Oh-kay," she says. That's how it sounds from her. Two separate, sharp little syllables. She's sweet. I like this girl. Not like that. I like her. I like that she's the closest thing I have to a friend.

My phone starts to ring again.

I look at the screen, and it flashes up *Unknown Number*.

I try to think for a minute of anyone who would be urgently trying to contact me with an undisclosed identity. The only people that I can think of who might call me are my parents, my doctor, or Cally. I don't think that Mum or Dad would block their identity, so it seems unlikely it's them. The health centre is closed at weekend, so I doubt it's my doctor. Cally is here, very obviously not using her phone. Maybe it's someone from the uni. A lecturer or...I don't know, I can't think of anyone that it might logically be. I expect lecturers stick to Monday to Friday office hours. I have no clue.

I answer. My voice is terser this time.

"Hello."

The same background din. I think I can hear a train service announcement, but I don't catch the details. People. Noise. No one speaks.

"Who is this?"

There's a soft crackle on the line, as if the caller moved and brushed against the mouthpiece.

"Hello?"

This time it's the caller's turn to hang up. The line clicks and goes dead, leaving me holding a silent line to my ear.

"Weird," I say to Cally.

I tap a message to my mum.

Were you trying to call me?

I know that it will probably result in her actually making a call, but at least I'll know if my mystery caller is Mum pocket dialing me.

I don't feel comfortable anymore. I curl my legs under me, tucking them up on the sofa. I'm fidgety, stressed.

"You okay?" Cally says.

"Yeah. Just annoying innit," I say.

She nods. I guess we all get this kind of call. Sometimes there's nothing unusual about the unusual.

My ring tone bursts into life again. I snap my phone up and look at the screen. This time it says MUM, her number clear beneath it.

"Everything okay?" she says before I even get the chance to offer a *hello*.

"Yeah," I say. "I thought I had a missed call from you." I lie. I don't want to worry her. She worries enough about me already, why make it worse? One day she will worry so much that she'll end up getting Dad to drive her down here. I bristle at the thought.

"No, we've been out this morning love. Dad wanted to go to the garden centre, and you know what he's like."

They carry on with the same routine, the

same simple pleasures, the same life that they lived before I left. Why would it be any different?

She keeps me on the line filling in the minutiae of their day until halfway through the next episode of Chase MD. I'm half watching the television, not really concentrating on what Mum is saying, making the right noises at the right time.

I mouth *sorry* across at Cally, but she waves away the apology. She gets up and waves her mug at me: the universal sign for "would you like another brew?". I nod and hold out my cup.

By the time she gets back with coffee I've said goodbye to Mum, promising to call her soon. When I hang up there are two missed calls from *Unknown Number*. I press down the button to power off.

Heidi gets home at two and heads to her room for a nap. How I envy her. I used to think nothing of it, curling up in bed or on the sofa, or anywhere soft and warm, sleeping in the daytime. I can imagine her there in her room, trainers off and straight onto her bed. Under the duvet, eyes shut, straight to sleep. I may have had a long blink while I watched TV with Cally; that's all I expect to get today.

I go to my room, and decide to switch my

phone back on, see if there's been any more calls from The Unknown. It takes a few moments to power up. There's nothing new. No missed calls. No texts. A few spammy emails, which I ignore. I slide it to silent and lay it on the table, before I lay myself on my bed. I'm going to read for a while before Eamon comes home and we all start getting ready to go out. It never takes me long because, well, like I've said, I don't make that much of an effort. Slap on the slap. Pick something clean to wear. Done.

I'm reading a psychological thriller about a woman who is lost in the woods. One benefit of my insomnia is that I have lots of extra time to read. It doesn't really matter if I read books that might give me nightmares now either, seeing as I don't sleep.

That was a half-joke. When I do doze, I can have micro-dreams during my micro-sleeps. Sometimes I'm not quite sure if I'm remembering dreams or actual memories. Things get muddled.

I keep glancing over at my phone, expecting it to start chirping at any moment, but it doesn't. I was annoyed when it was ringing, but the silent threat of the potential ringing is equally, if not more, frustrating.

By the time I start to get ready for our night out, my phone still hasn't rung again. I guess it was just someone pocket dialing me, but I can't work out who. Weird. One of those things. The great mysteries of life.

We are in the bar early enough to get a table, but certainly not the first people here. There's already a hum of chatter and the heat of warm bodies is steaming the windows.

Even though I'm not drinking, and the others are, we've agreed to buy drinks in rounds. To be honest, Coke is almost as expensive as the bottles of beer they are throwing back. The only issue I really have is that they are drinking theirs more quickly than I am. I'm not drinking to get drunk, so it's probably not quite as fun for me to keep throwing back the syrupy sweet drinks.

"They don't drink in Yorkshire?" Eamon asks. He's smiling, like it's a joke. I try to give him a little smile in return, but it won't come.

"I had a bad experience," I say. I hope that will be enough. His smile drops.

"Sorry, I didn't realise."

I know he didn't ask with any ill intent, but the atmosphere has soured with that one simple question. I'm grateful that he doesn't push it further.

"I don't mind getting yours though. Don't

worry about it," I say. I feel a bit sorry for him, ironically. He barely knows anything about me. Why would he know not to ask about why I don't drink?

"Sorry," he says, but I shake my head. "It's fine. Really. No drinking means no hangover anyway, right?"

He holds up his bottle, with the last dregs of his beer swishing at the bottom and clinks it against my Coke bottle. "I'll drink to that," he says.

I manage a smile now, even though he's not as funny as he thinks he is. He's a good guy though. Don't get me wrong. I like him.

"Another round?" I ask, first to him, and then to Heidi and Cally.

The girls are both ready too, so I squeeze from my seat and push through the crowd towards the bar.

We're so tightly packed, I feel the heat of the other bodies around me, the smell of sweat and breath and beer. I wish I were taller, that I could reach my head up above the crowd, inhale the air that circulates up there. I'm pressed against the back of a leather jacket, my T-shirt sliding up on it. I tug it down, back in position. I'm boxed in, my breaths start to quicken. Short, sharp intakes of hot air. My pulse thuds in my temples. I can't turn around and change my mind now, there's no way backwards. Nowhere to go but to keep, slowly, inching forwards.

Concentrate. Keep calm. Focus.

I feel a movement by my leg. I swat at it the best I can. I can barely move my arms, they're near flattened against me. My efforts have no effect. It feels like a fly or a wasp maybe, fuck...no. It's rhythmic, steady. I tentatively put my hand on the place I feel it, and realise my stupidity. It's my phone. I rarely keep it in my pocket. I'm not used to feeling this buzz, but still I feel like an idiot.

I try to tug it out, but I can't move, can't free it in time, and it falls silent. I've got my arm into an awkward position now; I have to jerk it back. I jab my elbow into the breast of a girl standing to my right side.

"Shit. Sorry," I say. She shrugs like it's normal, like it's just something that happens all the time.

I want to say something else, make a crack about how squashed in we are here, something about sardines in a can, but it feels more like we are pigs in a truck to the slaughterhouse.

Dontsaythatdontsaythatdontsaythat.

I don't say that.

I don't say anything. I rearrange my limbs

and try not to touch anyone more than I have to.

Eventually I surface at the bar. The guy in front of me squeezes off to the left, carrying two pints of lager in plastic cups that splash and spill over the girl standing in his path. She leans back, trying to let him through and steps on the foot of the girl behind her.

"Becky." A voice from behind. I whip my head around. I can't see anyone looking at me. No one is trying to get my attention.

I turn back to the bar.

"Miss?" The barman is staring at me, unimpressed. It's too busy here for me to be wasting anyone's time by phasing out.

Three Coronas, one Coke. I repeat it in my head, making sure I have it right before I ask. *Bottles*. Buying bottles means none of us has to carry four cupfuls back to the group.

"Becky." That voice again. To my left somewhere.

I look. There's a wave of people, but none of them appear to be calling to me. I don't recognise the voice. It's low, soft, female.

"Miss. Order or move along." The barman must have had a difficult shift and I'm not making it any easier here.

"I'm sorry," I say. "Coronas and a Coke,

please. Er, three Coronas. Bottles. And the Coke. A bottle, please."

Sharp and succinct. Smooth, Rebecca.

The barman looks at me like the dumbass I made myself out to be, then turns to the fridge to grab the drinks.

"Becky." Louder this time. From my right. Straight into my ear.

"What do you want?" I half-shout at the girl next to me.

"Oh, thanks. Uh…vodkacoke please."

I've never seen this girl before in my life.

"Were you just saying my name?" I ask in as loud a voice as I can manage without shouting.

She shakes her head.

"Miss. Your drinks. That's twelve eighty."

I hear the barman, and turn back to him.

"Sure," I say, tapping my debit card. The girl is out of luck for her *vodkacoke* tonight. I take the bottles by their necks, two in each hand, gripped between my fingers.

As I push my way through the mass, I keep looking around me. Ten, maybe eleven, thousand students at this university, and no one here that I recognise. If someone is looking for me, perhaps they will follow me, find me somewhere I can hear them and respond.

I get back to the guys and hand over their bottles.

"That took a while," Heidi says.

I point towards the bar, with its seven-deep queues.

"Fucking busy!" Eamon says. "Gets worse every week."

"More students turning to drink," I laugh, but I don't feel it. It's for them, not for me.

I remember the buzzing in my pocket, and fumble around for my phone. *Dear caller* is back. Unknown Number. You'd think people would have better things to do on a Saturday night. I put my phone on the table, next to my bottle, and try not to think about it.

Someone calling my name.

Someone ringing my phone.

Creepy coincidence? Or is someone playing games?

Chapter Nine

I try not to think about that night. Friday night. June 16th, 2018. I'll never forget it as long as I live. The problem is that every time I think about Jordan, I can't avoid thinking about how everything ended. And I think about him a lot.

Towards the end I guess I didn't see him as much as I did when we were younger. There were only two years between us, of course. Being similar ages probably helped. What helped more though was that he was a painfully shy child. I mean I'm introverted now, sure, but when I was a little kid, I would talk to anyone. Everyone. I wasn't selective. He latched onto me like I was the older one. Ironic really. If we went anywhere, he would wait for me to strike up a conversation or start playing with other kids, and then he would join in. As I got older, I distanced myself more from social interaction, but I could still hold a conversation when I had to. It was only after what happened at school that I became unwilling to talk to other people. Once bitten and all that.

Jordan changed when he met Jennie. She gave him confidence. The same kind of confidence that I had given him, I suppose. We were both crutches for him. He did everything for me though, so it was the least I could do for him. When I needed him, though…when all that shit happened in school, well…he wasn't there. He had started college already. It wasn't his fault, but still. I don't think they would have treated me like that. I don't think that it would all have happened the same way if Jordan had been there.

He said that he would go in with me, that he'd talk to them, sort them out. Whatever that meant. *Sort them out*, like he would put them in their place or something. I don't know what he could have done. Maybe nothing. Maybe that's why he didn't try.

It doesn't matter now.

When we were both at the same school, we would walk in together, walk home together, spend our breaks together. It must have been tough on him, looking back. He gave so much, and he never complained. It must have been a drag, having his kid sister tagging along after him all the time. Did I stop him from making his own friends? Did I hold him back? Did I ask too much of him?

I never thought about any of this at the time. I was happy that he was with me. I was happy that he was there for me. I never considered the cost.

When he went to college, I spent more time with Mischa. That's when we really stepped up our friendship. She was the one I was walking to and from school with. She was the one I spent my time with when we weren't in class. I guess we were close. I can see why people might have started those rumours about us. Maybe I would have thought those things about us too, if I was one of the other kids. I'm not saying it's right. I'm definitely not condoning the bullying. Funny how it was all aimed at me, and not Mischa, like I was the bad influence. I was the *weird* kid. They all felt sorry for her.

Eventually I had to feel sorry for her too, but for different reasons.

Within the year, before we sat our exams, before Jordan's accident, Mischa was dead.

I don't want to talk about it really. I mean, of course it didn't have the same effect on me as losing Jordan, but still, it stung. She had been my best friend, of course it fucking hurt.

How would I have felt if we were that close when she died?

How would I have coped?

Of course, if we had still been friends, if none of it had happened, the name calling, the bullying, the small-town narrow-minded bullshit, well I suppose she wouldn't be dead anyway.

Fuck. So many things that I don't want to think about.

I don't remember the date she died. It's not etched in my mind like the date of Jordan's death. Not that it didn't matter, I don't know, it just wasn't quite as important to me.

I do remember that they gave us the day off school. I sat in my room, alone, wondering why someone as great, as clever, as kind, as perfect as Mischa would kill themselves. I couldn't think of a reason. Nobody could.

When I talked to my psychiatrist about Mischa, I was amazed at how detached I could force myself to be. She had been my only real friend, apart from Jordan. An anomaly: someone who would happily spend time with me. Someone who valued my presence. Still, when I talked to Doctor Balliol, what came out was a list of questions.

"Why do you think someone like Mischa would take her life?" I asked.

Balliol looked at me, without answering, and wrote something on her pad. She always held onto that notebook, like it was her comfort blanket or something. She filled the pages with her observations, and probably her comments about her crazy patient, Rebecca Braithwaite.

"I mean...what do you think?" I asked.

She wouldn't be drawn though. I couldn't get her to fill in the gaps for me. I think she knew. I think she always knew.

"I'm interested, Rebecca, in why you are asking me," she said, eventually. It wasn't a question, so I didn't give her an answer.

She wrote something else and sat back in her chair. A lot of our sessions were spent in silence. I hated them. I hated every single one.

She had no answers for me, and I had none for her. Neither of us were willing to fill in the gaps, so we hung in silent stasis. I thought it was better than talking, but looking back, perhaps I should have engaged with her more. Perhaps I should have let her help me. I was bobbing on the surface then, and I thought that I could carry on treading water. Instead, over the months, I have sunk deeper. Instead of reaching out for the life preserver, I have let myself begin to drown. I no longer believe that I deserve to be saved.

Chapter Ten

Monday morning, I'm in class with Cally. We got here earlier this time, and landed seats in the middle of the room. I haven't tripped over anyone yet today. I managed to eat breakfast. It's looking like a good day.

About ten minutes into the session, my lecturer is in full flow, running us through a slide show and giving her full-on animated discussion of popular creative non-fiction. I'm scribbling down notes, when my phone starts to vibrate with an incoming call.

I try to ignore it. I feel it against my leg, but I know that no one else will know where it's coming from. Maybe Cally, next to me, no one else. I keep my pen in my hand, my eyes on my lecture notes.

The buzz continues for what feels like minutes, but no one has drawn attention to it, so I don't either. I let it continue, trilling away to itself. Fuck it. Whoever is doing this must get bored soon.

The lecturer is giving an in-detail description of Capote's *"In Cold Blood"*. I read it for A-Levels, but I don't raise my hand when she asks a question. Sometimes, I just can't be bothered. My lethargy makes me so apathetic sometimes. Often. Usually. I try to concentrate as the lecturer discussed the way the author manipulates the reader's sympathies. Can you feel sympathy for a murderer? I did, when I read the book. I was manipulated for certain. It's an interesting question. Do we only see the side of people that we are shown, and accept that surface as the truth, or should we dig deeper?

The vibration in my bag stops. I feel my shoulders sag. I hadn't even realised I was so tense, that the calls were affecting me so much, but now it has ended, I feel the relief. The pause is only momentary, as the buzz-ringing starts again.

Cally looks at me and gives a subtle nod downwards towards my bag. She has noticed then. I pass back the tiniest shrug. I don't want to do anything about it. I don't want to be pressured. All those calls on Saturday. I'm not going to keep answering just to be greeted by silence.

"Turn it off," she says in a hushed tone that's not quite a whisper.

I flash my eyes over to the lecturer, and see that she is looking back at me. No hiding anymore. I mouth "sorry" and reach down into my bag. I try to fish around without looking, trying to create as little a disruption as possible to the lecture. I can't get my hand on it.

I huff out an annoyed sigh, pull my bag onto

my lap and open it properly.

There it is. Its glowing face flashes "Unknown Number".

I could squeeze past the row of students to my right and go outside, answer my phone. I could turn it off and try to feign ignorance.

I know that it's going to be stuck on my mind though, that I won't be able to just forget about it. Everything is stacking up, niggling in my head. The pressure is building. Fuck I need to sleep. I need sleep so very badly.

I opt to turn my phone off, if only because I can't bear to make a show of myself by disturbing eight other students who are trying to focus on class, just so I can answer this - probably silent - call. I stuff my phone into my bag, and push my bag back down onto the floor.

I see Cally's bemused expression. I choose to ignore that too.

After the lecture she asks what I'm up to next, and I make a crappy excuse. I want to be on my own the next time my phone rings. I'm going to answer next time. I'm going to have it out with my mystery caller. I can't let this carry on. Cally gives me a suspicious look, but lets me go.

I head back to my room, and start to look

through my lecture notes. Believe it or not, despite everything that has happened, and everything that is happening, I want to do well on this course. I want to study. I want to put in the hours. I want the good grades.

Journalism: it was Jordan's dream job. He was on the student newspaper at college, always writing bits and pieces about absolutely anything. Even before that, I remember him interviewing me, years back, writing in a wire-bound reporter's notepad with his red chunky Beryl handwriting pen. He'd flip open the cover, and sit with pen poised and an earnest expression on his face, like I was some big shot celebrity he was getting the scoop on. What's your favourite colour? What's your favourite biscuit? Who's your favourite brother?

I want this. I want this for him. I want it for me. I don't know, maybe a part of me thinks that if I do this. If I can get through this course, if I can pass, then somehow, I'll feel better. Perhaps this is what I need to be able to move on, to move forwards with my life. It's honouring his memory, somehow, living his dream. I never really had one of my own. Like I said, I toyed with the idea of studying psychology, but I don't know, it was never something I was really going to do. I wasn't passionate about it, not like Jordan was with his journalism.

At first, my psychiatrist, dear Doctor Balliol, tried to talk me out of coming to university. *It's too much for you. Too much pressure. You're in no fit state. You need to carry on with your therapy. I can't discharge you. This isn't good for you.* So much negativity. Like she didn't want me to do something good for once. Give me the chance, just one time; let me do something right.

Then I started to talk. After months of being an impenetrable shell, I started to open up; I started to share more with her. The more I talked, the more I told her about everything, the more she softened. She started to warm to the idea of me moving forwards, having something to focus on. It wasn't long before she started to support my plans. In the end, it was her who spoke to my parents, telling them that university could be *a positive move for Rebecca.*

Oh, I came on so far in those final sessions. I was a changed woman. That's what she said. Had anything changed though? Had *I* changed? Or was I just telling Balliol what she wanted to hear?

My phone rings, just as I knew it would.
Unknown number.

Those two words flash on and off.

I put my pen down, pick my phone up, and listen.

Indistinct noise. Static. Voices. Distant. Traffic. A city?

I say nothing. My caller says nothing.

A car horn blares. A woman shouts in the background, nothing to do with the call.

Nothing identifiable. Nothing that tells me who is calling or where they are.

"Who is this?" I have to be the first to speak.

I can hear breathing at the other end of the line. Steady. Confident.

"What is it? What the hell do you want?"

This gets a response. At last, something. From the other end of the line I hear laughter. Thick, heavy laughter.

"Yeah. Funny. Fuck off."

I hang up.

Someone from home? That's what I'm thinking. It's been a long time since anyone gave me any trouble. All that stuff in high school, it stopped after what happened with Jordan. People left me alone after that. It was like I had gone through enough, I suppose, without all their shit on top of it. How could they have made me feel any worse after what happened? Besides, I had pretty much left school then, when Jordan died. I did my final exams and I was out of there.

I got Mum and Dad to let me go to a college out of town. I didn't want to be with those bitches anymore. I wanted to be away from all of that, away from all the nastiness, away from anyone who knew me, or at least thought they did. Mum was so pleased that I wanted to carry on and do my A-levels, after everything. I could have just played on their sympathy and lounged around in depression for a few months, years, whatever. Fuck that. I wanted to get on with life. I owed that to my brother.

Now this. Some idiot thinks it's funny to call me up, mess with my head. What do they want from me? What can they possibly get from winding me up? Some people are just straight up twisted. I would love to think it was a mistake, or a wrong number, but now, after the laughter, I can't convince myself that it's not personal.

Still, I have been getting more and more paranoid recently. There was the incident with my coat and bag, and how I had been almost certain that there was someone in the room. Then the girl in the café who had simply recognised me from our first week here. I have been overreacting a lot. I can see that. I make a mental note to mention it to Doctor Fisher when I go back for my medication review. Maybe the new meds I'm on are doing more harm than good. One thing is for certain: they are not helping me to sleep.

Chapter Eleven

I don't have any lectures for the rest of the day, so I chill for a while in the lounge and then get ready to go to the library.

The building is a five-storey monster. Grey concrete, designed with its purpose in mind, rather than aesthetics. The ground floor has an open area, with the enquiry desk at its centre. There are study areas, tables with plain plastic chairs around them, side rooms with the group working spaces; these are quieter, more conducive to concentration. In the main area, students chat to each other, tap away at their laptops, and listen to music on their phones that leaks from their earbuds in a tinny unidentifiable stream. There are two vending machines, one for snacks and another for cans or bottles of drinks. You could probably live in here. It's open twenty-four hours, so maybe some people do. It's cheaper than paying rent.

My personal preference is to skip the ground floor and head up to Third. That's where all the course books for my degree are. Like I said, most of it is online, but I still enjoy referring directly to the hard copy sometimes. I can concentrate better on paper. I get so easily distracted that I do anything I can to make it as simple as I can for myself. I was told that I could have something called Additional Learning Support, but they wanted me to sign a form to say they could share my information with other organisations, and I didn't want that. I don't want professionals discussing me. I don't want to become a case number or That Girl Who Can't Sleep. I want to get on with my life.

I walk along the centre aisle of books, and pull out the textbook I need. There's something pleasing about the solid weight of it. I can learn everything I would ever need to know by doing a Google search on my phone, but that doesn't have the same *feel* as browsing through a book for the answers. If you love books, you'll understand.

I choose a desk as far away from the entrance to the floor as possible. I don't want to be disturbed by other people coming and going. I pick a window seat, more for the natural light than for the view. It's turned out to be a rainy, miserable day. The sky is a washed out, pale, pathetic blue, dappled with charcoal grey clouds. I'm glad to be inside, even if I am studying.

I pull out my laptop; and I start to work. My eyes flit from the words I'm typing on the screen to the words in the textbook. Every now and again I see movement out of the window and turn my head to gaze outside.

Most of my classmates seem to spend their off-time either in the student union building, or they head into town to the shops and the bars. I spend a fair amount of time in the SU, but my inability to sleep gives me many more hours to spend than other people. I'm time-rich, sleep-poor. You could see it as a positive thing that I get all these extra hours in the day. If I wanted to look on the bright side, that's about the only bright side there is.

Even from my carefully positioned distance, I suddenly hear the doors to the floor open and then slam shut. The noise echoes through the emptiness. I look around in annoyance at the interruption, but I can't see anyone, they must have changed their mind. I turn back to the screen and carry on with my work.

One of my assignments this term is to write an editorial piece for the journal of my choice. It's only an exercise, we don't actually have to submit it. Maybe I'll make some use of it anyway. I want to write something about what I'm going through; I'm planning to write about insomnia.

I type three words onto the screen:

I can't sleep

I watch the cursor ticking away, a single vertical line flashing on-off-on-off. It's hypnotic.

There's another bang of the door and I whirl around more quickly this time. Still I see nothing. The words on the screen stare at me, bidding me to continue, inviting me to write, to share my story, to share my pain.

From my left, just behind the nearest bookshelf, I hear a dull thud.

Then another.

And a third.

Clearly someone didn't read the signs about being quiet in the library. As a fourth thump sounds, I get up and walk to the end of the aisle of books. I'm about to say something, but there's no one there to say anything to. The aisle is empty, apart from four large books, stacked neatly on top of each other in the centre.

From a few aisles over, I hear another thud. Two. Three. What the fuck? I dart to the end of the shelf and pop my head around. No one. A pile of books in the middle. I shake my head. I don't like leaving my laptop and my bag like this. I don't like running around the library like an idiot. I feel as though someone is playing a trick on me, but I don't know anyone here well enough for them to want to. No one except Cally, and she doesn't seem the sort to do something stupid like this.

"Can you stop, please?" I say in my loudest, most stern voice.

There are another two thuds in response.

"Oh, fuck off," I shout.

I don't even bother going to see where the books are being dropped this time. Whoever wants to play this game can do it on their own. I'm not interested in wasting my energy. I walk back over to my desk and sit back at my laptop. When I look down, I freeze, and then I almost vomit.

Below where I typed "I can't sleep" are five words. Five words that I didn't type.

Then I see something else. Tucked beneath the corner of my laptop is a piece of paper. I see the edge of it, a jagged rip. I tug at it, pull it out so I can see it properly. It's got something written on it.

I frown, trying to make sense of it. Trying to make sense of all of this. Someone lured me over to the shelves so they could run to my desk and leave me a message?

Stop.

Think.

I haven't heard any more noise since those final thuds. I haven't heard the doors open and close again. Whoever it is must still be here.

"This isn't funny," I call out.

It only struck me after the books started to thud that I'm the only student on this floor. At least I *was* alone. Looks like I'm not now.

"Why don't you just show yourself? You fucking chicken shit bastard." My voice gets louder until, by the end of the sentence, I'm near screaming. I set off along the edge of the shelves, looking down each aisle, half running, and hyped up on adrenaline. "Fuck you. Come out."

I'd rather face off with whoever it is than be fucked around with like this. If I need to, I can run out of here. There are staff downstairs, and students on other floors. If I need help, I can get it.

"Come on." I extend the *n* in an anguished howl.

This is bullshit.

Then I hear it: the door opens, the door slams shut. They're leaving. They came in here, fucked with me and now they are leaving.

I race over to the entrance and tear the door back open. I can't see anyone. The stairwell is empty. The lift shows number five in its red digital glow. I must have gotten here like six seconds after whoever just left. They didn't have time to go anywhere. I look down the staircase, then up the staircase. There's no sign of anyone running or even walking. There's no one else here.

I run down the stairs towards Ground. It's a spur of the moment decision, and I'm mindful that I've left my laptop and my belongings unattended on Third. Who am I looking for? What am I going to do if I find someone?

When I make it to the bottom, I open the door into Ground. Everything looks peaceful and still. I do the first thing that comes to my mind: ask a librarian. I stand in front of the enquiry desk, breathless and sweaty, and lean in to the assistant.

"Can I help you?" she asks. Her tone is flat like she would rather be anywhere else than at her desk, dealing with me.

"Did someone run through here? Someone was…er, I mean…I've come from Third. I was trying to study, and someone was throwing books around. They messed with my laptop."

"You need to take responsibility for your personal belongings and *valuables* at all times in the library," she says. Even the suggestion that someone might have been damaging books doesn't rouse her.

"Did you see anyone? Anyone suspicious?" I ask.

"What does *suspicious* look like?" She's almost mocking me, barely containing her condescension.

Fuck off. I think.

"I don't know. I guess you'd know it if you saw it." I guess if someone had run down the stairs into the lobby, they would try to make themselves look as *normal* as possible, and try to blend in with the other students. I don't expect they would want to draw attention to themselves, unless they were stupid.

"Maybe I would. But no. Nothing *suspicious.*" Her tone is so droll, it winds me up even more.

"Great. Thanks for your help."

I have no real choice other than to give up. There's no evidence of anyone acting strangely here, and I'm hyperaware that my laptop and bag are on Third.

Take responsibility for your personal belongings and valuables.

It sounds like a good idea.

I head back upstairs, and half expect to see something else typed onto my screen. There is nothing new. Everything seems to be as I left it when I ran downstairs. I read the note again.

The books are for you.

It's a neat note, written in black biro. I can't

tell if the handwriting is male or female, as the lettering is small and generic. There are no immediate clues as to the author. I turn it over in my hand, but there's nothing on the reverse, and the paper is entirely unremarkable.

Fuck. I can't believe I'm being so calm about it. The books are for me. Well thank you. Great. I guess I'll put them away then. Fucker.

My body is still trembling with adrenaline. Whoever did this is long gone, but I still feel like I'm being watched. I'm always on edge, always at the mercy of my frayed, sleep-starved nerves, but this is different. Whoever did this *knows* me. When I read those words on the screen, I knew it. That's what *really* freaked me out. The fact that someone had gotten my attention and then crept over to type on my screen and leave me a note is freaky in itself, sure, but it was personal. It was meant specifically for me. It wasn't just an opportunistic prankster. Someone knows me and someone is messing with me. Really messing with me. Prank calls. Shouting my name in the bar. This.

Fuck.

As I bend to pick up the books, I see further confirmation that someone really is dicking me about. The texts have been carefully selected to send me a message. The first four, closest to where

I was sitting, are all textbooks about the effects of insomnia. The second and third piles are similarly themed. In the final aisle, there's a single book, lying on its own in the centre of the walkway between the shelves. This one isn't a textbook. It's a hardback book, solid and heavy. Its cover is a mid-blue, with the faded image of a boy's face. It looks like a psychological thriller. I can tell by the typeface. The cover looks like all the other books from the genre. I read a lot, and I read a lot of these particular kinds of books. I have never heard of this title though.

I stand and stare at it. The book has been positioned so that I can see the cover, see the picture and see the title. It's the title that really stabs me.

You Killed Him.

"Fuck off!" I yell, although I'm sure there's no one here to hear me. Not the person who did this, anyway. "Leave me alone. Just fuck off. It was an accident! It wasn't my fault. It wasn't..." I break off the sentence as my voice turns to sobs. I can't bear to think about it, not like this. Who the fuck is doing this to me?

I don't put the book back on the shelf. Instead I give it a swift sharp kick, and it skids along the thin, cheap carpet and slams along the far wall beneath the shelving unit.

"Fuck you," I say, under my breath, "just fuck you."

I've been trying to hold it together, but as I head back to the desk where I left my belongings, I can't control myself. Coming to university here, so far away, was meant to help me to get away from all that, from everything. From everyone. I wanted a new start. I can't handle this. I slump back into the seat by my laptop, lower my face into my hands, and let the tears flow.

When I have emptied my heart, I take a big, snotty breath and release a long, deep sigh. I have to get it together. I have to...

What the fuck?

When my eyes fix on my laptop screen, all I see are the three words that I wrote:

I can't sleep

The words that were typed beneath have been deleted. The hand-written note has also gone. I know I left it here, on top of my keyboard. I know I did.

I push my hands into the pockets of my jacket, double checking, doubting myself. I search through the many pockets of my jeans. I lift up the textbook, checking beneath it and then holding it by its spine, letting the pages fall like a fan.

Nothing.

I check beneath the laptop. I get on my hands and knees and shine the light from my mobile phone over the floor. If there was a piece of white paper on this dull, drab navy-blue carpet I would be able to see it, but I can't. It's not here. It's as if it melted out of existence.

I get up to my feet again, and slam my hands down on the desk. This is so fucked-up. I should go to Security. But what would I tell them? Someone left a message on my laptop and then deleted it. Someone left a note for me and then came back and took it? I could imagine how Security would respond.

-And what did the note say, ma'am?

-"The books are for you"

-Not exactly a death threat is it? And what books were they?

-They were all relevant to the assignment that I'm writing.

-A helpful poltergeist, maybe?

I imagine them laughing. I imagine myself not telling them about the final book, and definitely not wanting to tell them what was typed on the laptop screen. You don't need to know. I don't want to repeat it. I don't want to tell Security.

I start to scoop my belongings up into my

bag, all the time thinking about what I should do next. After the episode last night, and now this, I think that seeing my doctor is a good place to start. There are only two people at this university that know about Jordan: Doctor Fisher and Cally. I can't believe that Cally would have anything to do with this, but how well do I know her? I shouldn't have talked. I shouldn't have said anything. I shouldn't have let myself start to believe that I could have a fresh start, with friends, with a future.

Chapter Twelve

On my walk back to South my edginess has me stopping every few metres to look over my shoulder. I find myself seeing shapes in shadows, imagining that everyone who looks at me is staring. More than that, their glances feel like judgements. All of these people, these strangers, of course they don't know me. They don't know anything about me. Still, I feel their eyes branding my skin.

I walk more quickly than usual and when I get to the main entrance of South, I fumble the numbers to the code-lock. A red error message flashes up and for a moment I can't remember how to reset it to try again. It comes to me, slowly, and I type the correct numbers in carefully. The door clicks open and I give it a relieved shove.

Back in the flat, the lounge is empty, and I pop my head around to the kitchen. There's no one there.

I've been thinking about this all the way home: I have to talk to Cally. Of course, if she did have something to do with what happened in the library, she's not likely to admit to it. I have to think everything through, I have to try to piece things together.

Cally. Would she do this? Why would she? She wouldn't. Would she? I'm not certain of anything.

Meanwhile, I'm going to phone the health centre and check back in with Doctor Fisher. I don't know how I'm going to broach things with her either. I don't want her thinking...well, I don't want to have to go to a shrink again. This isn't my fault. None of this is my fault. I'm trying to get away from it, but somehow, it's following me. I don't ever want to forget Jordan, but please, let me get over what happened.

I round the corner into the corridor where Cally's room and mine are. As I pass her door, the light glinting off the mirror in the bathroom opposite catches my eye, and I look in. I look like shit. I mean I always appear drawn and exhausted, but today, fuck, I look bad. I rub my eyes, and Mirror-Me rubs her eyes. I feel bad that my reflection has to be stuck with me. She could do better. I splash some cold water onto my face and wipe it with a towel. Great. I feel...exactly the same. I realise that I haven't even had micro-sleeps today. I've been active all day, and what with everything that happened at the library, my brain is fried.

When I push the door open into my room

all I want to do is lie on my bed and pass out. The bed looks so welcoming. I've tried to make it that way. I want to trick my mind into believing that *bed* is a good place to be. I wanted to set up my room so that it is clear and clean and uncluttered, because that's what the books say. Some of the books that were stacked up *for me* in the library probably contained that top tip. I prickle with frustration and anger and...I don't even know what it is, this other feeling. Fear? There's definitely some fear. The fear of not knowing what the fuck happened today, and the fear of not knowing whether it's going to happen again.

Who is fucking with me?

I manage to convince myself not to hit my bed straight away, and instead, I sit at my desk, and take out my phone. I flick through the contacts until I get to *Health Centre* and click to make the call.

The next appointment with Doctor Fisher is in two days. I take it.

It's another hour before I hear people in the living room. I can hear Eamon's voice booming, but I can't work out what he's saying from here. I didn't resist my bed for long, and I've been splayed out, spatchcock style, flicking through my phone. I've spent my time thinking, and overthinking, and then trying not to think. It's a vicious, very vicious, circle.

My head is heavy and thick like a clogged drain. I would rather stay here, rest it against my pillow, keep thinking, stay immobile, inert, but I want to talk to Cally. I get up, and I realise that my head is even more foggy than I thought, and I stumble to my side. I knock the alarm clock onto the floor in my clumsiness as I bang my hip into the bedside table. I rub at the place that I expect a purple bruise to bloom over the next few hours.

Idiot.

I put the clock back in place and head into the living room, cursing myself under my breath.

Fucking clumsy idiot.

Heidi and Cally are sitting together on a single sofa; Eamon is standing in the centre of the room, two mugs in one hand, one in the other.

"Want a coffee?" he asks. "I was just going to make some."

When I first started with the insomnia, I tried to avoid caffeine. It was one of the suggestions from my GP.

Cut caffeine.

Try to avoid unnecessary stimulation before bedtime.

Don't look at screens for an hour before you go to bed.

I tried all of those things, and many more, but none of them seemed to make the blindest bit of difference. I did give it a whole six months of drinking that decaffeinated crap, believe me. Eventually, I thought *what the hell* and went back to my five-cup-a-day regular coffee habit.

"Yeah," I say. "My mug's in the kitchen." Then I think for a split second and add, "I'll give you a hand."

He shrugs and we both go into the kitchen.

"It's been pretty quiet here this afternoon," I say as he opens the cupboard, pulls out the mugs.

"We went down to the supermarket. I knocked on your door, but you must have been out?"

"Oh? What time?" This is easier than I thought it would be.

"Must have been about two. We stopped for burgers on the way back. You know what Heidi's like."

I do. Sounds like our standard shopping trips. Buy a load of food to cook and then get a takeaway.

"Just the two of you?"

"Cally too. She got some of these..." He

pulls a box of teabags out of the cupboard and waves them at me. Yorkshire Tea. It's the tea that Mum buys, and a burst of mixed emotions blossoms in my mind.

"That's cool. I'll make us all one later," I smile. My smile fades when I remember that I was blaming Cally, in my mind, for what happened today. Maybe not blaming. Maybe just suspecting. "I'm sorry I missed out. I was in the library."

"Getting ahead of the game. Good work. You have lots on then?"

"Shitloads. So much." I feel more relaxed now. Something about being able to chat about normal, everyday things is calming.

Eamon is studying...actually, I can't remember the title of his course. It's one of those degrees that sounds made-up. Social anthromorphism or something.

"What's your course called again?" I ask him.

"Biological anthropology," he grins.

Like I said.

He pours the water into the mugs, makes the coffees, and we carry two each back in to the girls.

"Thanks for getting that tea, Cal," I say, as I hand over her drink.

"No worries." She raises her mug in a little *cheers* gesture.

All the time that I was in the library, these three were together, at the supermarket. It sounds such a droll, simple explanation for Cally's whereabouts, but I have no reason to doubt it.

I'm still shaken by the events of the afternoon, but I don't know what I can do about it. Perhaps it will be a one-off. It could have been someone trying to get a reaction out of me, for whatever warped reason. Well, they certainly succeeded. I hope they are happy.

No. I don't at all; I hope they rot in hell.

I stay in the lounge with my flat mates for the rest of the evening. Before I came to uni, I isolated myself a lot, spent too much time on my own, in my room. After Mischa, and then Jordan, I gave up on other people. I have so many nighttime hours alone now that I've started forcing myself to spend daylit hours being more social. I don't find it easy, but it's different, somehow, with these three.

Although I'm closest to Cally, Heidi is a warm and bubbly girl. I think her parents were some kind of hippies; she's all peace and love and incense. Not that those are bad things. If I wasn't so fucked-up and totally disinterested in relationships, she would probably be my type. I don't think about it too much. I don't like to think about anything that my sleep deprivation has deprived me of.

Eamon fits into the otherwise female group with an ease that comes from growing up alongside two sisters. From the day we moved in, he has never complained once about being placed here with the three of us. We are equals, and we rub along happily. I wouldn't go as far as to say that we are a team, it's only been three weeks since we met, but we are a happy, balanced group. I guess that's why being with them is calming and comforting. No one is going to be fucking with me while I am sitting here with my flatmates. I think I can count on them to look out for me. I hope that I don't have to.

Obviously, it's still on my mind, what happened in the library. How could it not be? On the surface I'm sure I look calm and controlled, but underneath I'm bubbling, like a pan of milk simmering on the hob. Any second, any slight increase in heat, and I could boil over, out of control. I can feel it, that tension.

When the other three go to their rooms, each heading towards several hours of deep, unbroken sleep, I am left alone with only my thoughts to occupy myself.

I think about the library, the books, and the useless librarian but most of all I think about what was written on the screen.

Whilst the main focus of my appointments with Doctor Balliol was my insomnia, we also spent a long time working through the guilt I felt over what happened to Jordan. I didn't engage with her for a long time. I didn't want to talk about what happened. For the first month solid, I would turn up for the sessions and sit in silence, staring at my boots, or picking at my nails, or finding something in the room fascinating enough to focus on rather than answering Balliol's questions.

I'm surprised she left it four weeks before she invited my parents in to discuss my lack of engagement.

"Do what it takes," my dad told her.

"In order for any kind of therapy to be of use to the patient, they have to participate," Balliol said, leaning towards my parents. "Rebecca and I have had four appointments now, and I haven't got anything from her other than grunted *hellos* and *goodbyes*."

That's something, I thought, but didn't say. I just kept up the old routine.

Don't respond.

Don't do this.

They can't make me do this.

But then I saw my mum's face. The tears falling down her sunken cheeks, from eyes ringed with the same darkness that mine have now. I read on her face the sheer grief, and heartbreak that I hadn't taken the time to recognise before. I had lost sight of the fact that she was suffering too. I was so caught up in my own feelings, my own emotion, that I had never stopped to consider that she was going through her own hell.

I had her and my father to lift me up, to try to carry me through it. She had no one. I made assumptions, pieced together fragments of things that I heard, things that I saw. Their relationship, my parents, it suffered. Neither of them was the same after Jordan. Their marriage was definitely not the same. Our home went from being a warm place of comfort and happiness to something like a cave: cold, dark and empty.

"There must be something you can do to help her," Mum said. Her voice cracked; the pain bled through. As much as I wanted to keep my thoughts and feelings and my own personal, unbearable aching to myself, I had to do something to make things better for her. All I could do was try to engage with Balliol, to try to get better. She had lost Jordan, and I realised that to some extent she felt that she had lost me too.

I put my hand out onto hers.

"Don't," I said. "I'll try harder. For you. I promise. I'll try."

Doctor Balliol nodded slowly, and her face formed a genuine, warm smile.

I did it for her. For Mum. I opened up when all I wanted to do was to close down, and shut myself off completely. I thought that without Jordan there was nothing left to live for, that nothing was important anymore, but I was wrong. There was Mum. I had college, I had Jordan's dreams to fulfil, and I wasn't going to get anywhere moping around, making everyone feel like shit.

I suppose a part of me thought that when I started to offload all of the emotional pain and guilt that I might start to be able to sleep again. It had no effect at all. I didn't feel any better. I didn't sleep any better.

Mum hugged me, but Dad was standing up to leave before we had even booked the next appointment. I'm not saying he didn't care, or that he doesn't care, I'm just not sure that he believes in psychiatry. He doesn't think that talking can help with anything. I guess that's why he and Mum have drifted so far apart. Maybe he was worried about the money. We weren't a take-two-kids-on-holiday-to-America rich, and we weren't pay-for-a-private-psychiatrist rich, but they paid, and I carried on going, trying a little harder, but never feeling any better.

Chapter Thirteen

I leave my room early the next morning to head for my appointment at the health centre. The receptionist had sounded hesitant when she told me the only slot they had was at eight-thirty, but I don't get the lie-ins that other students do. Eight-thirty is as good a time as any for me, and I was relieved to get an appointment so soon.

I'm shown straight through to Fisher's office, and I smile and sit down on the chair she offers me.

"Rebecca, hello. How did you get on with your new tablets?"

The doctor is facing me directly, swiveled in my direction, fully focused. It's quite a contrast to my uncomfortable shuffling. I hate talking about myself.

"Not great," I say.

I've rehearsed how I am going to describe what happened in the library. Now that I'm sitting here, I'm wondering if it has anything to do with the sleeping pills at all.

"Okay..." She prompts me and waits for me to speak.

I take a breath, and begin.

"They haven't help me to sleep."

"Sometimes it can take a little while for them to get into the system," she says, in a soft, reassuring tone.

"Something else though. I've been feeling some symptoms that I think might be related to the meds. Like, paranoid, edgy kind of."

"Anything specific?"

I hum and sigh, and get to the point.

"First off, I had an episode, in the middle of the night, where I thought my coat and bag were someone standing in my room." I give a little laugh, so she knows that I know this is nuts. "And then...I thought someone was stalking me in the library." I pause. "I think someone was. I don't know. Probably. I mean, they were. Yes."

"If someone *was* stalking you, that's not a medical issue. It's not something to do with your medication, it's something you should talk to Security about." She's deadly serious. I don't know what response I expected.

I start to describe what happened.

"I was working in the library. I was on my own. I heard some banging and when I went to look there were piles of books on the floor. I couldn't see anyone around that had dropped them. It seemed, well, I felt like someone did it on purpose, to get my attention. I went back to my desk and someone had typed something on the screen while I was off looking around. And...they left a note under my laptop."

It sounded a lot less threatening when I described it like that.

She's looking at me, expecting more.

"That's it," I say. "I ran downstairs, but I couldn't see anyone suspicious, and the librarian was no help."

"What did *they* write? What did the note say?"

"'The books are for you'," I say.

"Do you still have it? Maybe, if you're worried, you should take it to Security and explain all of this."

"Um, no. When I went back to my laptop, I mean, when I opened my eyes...when..." What did happen? I try to remember what had happened to the note. "It had gone. And the words on the screen...they were gone too."

"When you opened your eyes?"

"Yeah, I sat back down at the desk and I..."

What had happened? I had put my head in my hands, and maybe I closed my eyes, maybe just for a minute. Maybe for longer. Perhaps *this* is why my instinct told me not to go straight to Security.

"Do you think there's a chance that you...that you might have been asleep? Do you think you had a micro-sleep?"

She doesn't say *that you imagined this* or *that you dreamt this*. I'm grateful for that, but I think it's what she means.

"The books though. I put them away. I picked them up and carried them back to the shelves. I remember doing it. I definitely moved the books. At least...I'm fairly sure I did. Well, apart from one. I..." I don't want to admit it, but I don't think she's going to inform on me to the librarians. "I kicked it under the shelf, near the wall."

She gives me a quizzical look. I'm not sure she is buying any of this. The more I say, the more I doubt myself too.

"It was..." I sigh and come out with it. "The book was called *'You Killed Him'*. I felt like someone was trying to get at me. Because of Jordan, you know."

"And the other books...?"

"They were all about sleep deprivation, insomnia and that kind of thing. That's what I am writing my assignment about. Write what you know." I try to smile, but I can't quite manage it.

She nods and picks her words deliberately. "All of the things that happened...everything that you have described...these things are linked to what's going on in your life, and in your thoughts, at the moment. One of the side effects of this drug is that sometimes it is possible for people to just *lose* time. Do you think that, maybe, that could have happened?"

I'm already nodding back in agreement. Paranoia. Imagining things. Dreaming. She could be right.

I'm also thinking about the book that I kicked under the shelf. If I *didn't* imagine everything, if it wasn't a dream, the book will still be there. No one would have known I kicked it there into the darkness and dust. No one would have retrieved it.

"Yes," I say to the doctor. "Maybe."

She turns to the screen and taps in some words.

"I'd like to refer you to someone, if you consent," she says.

Here we go. Back into therapy. I didn't want this. I don't want this.

"I think you need to work on the feelings that you have." I start to interrupt but she raises her hand to stop me. "I know you don't want to, and I know you have been in th- I know you have seen a specialist before...but these symptoms you're experiencing...well, I think talking to someone could help. And we will stop those drugs."

That's something.

"Will you give me something else? Something different?"

She purses her lips and draws in air, as though she was sucking through a straw.

"I think we will give you a break from them for a while." She clocks my disappointed expression and continues. "You've said yourself that none of the drugs have helped. Perhaps we should make you an appointment to see Doctor Brightside and see if we can tackle it from that direction."

It's a scary thought, existing without medication, but as I think about it, I can't see why it should be. If nothing has worked then maybe I'm best without anything. Perhaps seeing a psychiatrist again, and being invested in it, committed to it...perhaps that's how I will finally find out how to sleep again.

"Okay," I say, quietly.

When my GP back home first recommended a referral, the waiting lists were months long. That's why I ended up with a private doctor. My parents wanted me to skip the queues, and to get seen as soon as possible. They wanted the best for me, I know. I expect it to be the same now. If I call my mum and tell her I want to go back into therapy, they will find the money, but I don't want to do that. I've been enough of a burden and a drain upon their emotions and resources.

"Luckily for you, Doctor Brightside is one of my dearest friends," Fisher says.

"That's actually his name?" I almost laugh. I thought Fisher was making some kind of joke when she had first said it.

"*Her* name, yes." The doctor smiles and there's a wave of light through this otherwise tense consultation. "Abigail Brightside. Great name for a psychiatrist. Some people are born for a particular job, I suppose."

I do let out a little laugh. It feels like honey in my mouth, sweet and heavy. Things have been so *dark*. I need this. I need something good to happen.

"I'll give her a call and see when we can get you in." She looks at the screen again. "I have your number here. Ends in 247?"

"That's the one."

"Okay, I'll call you when I have arranged everything. Stop taking the Somniclone. Have a think about what happened at the library. If you do believe that someone is trying to harm you in any way, go to Security. Okay? Straight away."

I nod.

This has felt like such a positive, uplifting meeting, despite the fact that I'm leaving knowing that I'm going to be headed back into therapy in the not-too-distant future. Things could change. Things can change.

When I leave the health centre I head up towards the library, rather than down, back home to South. I have to see it for myself. I have to know whether the book is there, under the shelf where I kicked it.

I get a prickle of nervous tension as I enter the library doors. Whether I dreamed everything or whether there was actually someone there taunting me, I still get a sick feeling in my gut as I walk up the stairs to Third. It's like returning to the scene of the crime, but surely, I was the victim.

The library is busier today. I saw a group of students waiting for the lift on the ground floor, and two guys have walked down the stairs past me as I've climbed up. I try to always take the stairs rather than the lift, but some days I don't have the energy. Some days I don't even have the energy to leave my room. I get by on minimal sleep, but, as I have said, sometimes it really is just getting by.

I push open the door to Third. There's a girl

at the table nearest the door, hood up, the trail of her earphones' cord connecting her umbilically to her mobile phone. I can hear the tinny tick of her music, but I can't identify the tune. She's swinging back on the rear legs of her chair, and flops the front legs down onto the floor to let me pass.

Near the window, where I was sitting when I was here last, there are two boys dressed in near-identical jeans and sweatshirt combos. They are hunched over one of the laptops, watching a video. I can see something flickering, and I can hear the noise that they aren't bothering to keep at a reasonable level for the other library users. The other library user; apart from the girl and me, they are the only people on this floor. I'm glad they are all here though. I don't think I would have liked walking around here on my own. It's creeping me out being back here at all. Nothing bad happens when other people are around...right? Unless they are the ones making bad things happen, but that seems like it would be a huge coincidence.

I walk along the back shelves, trying to look nonchalant, like I'm trying to locate a book. I am trying to locate a book, of course, just not on the shelf. I trail my finger along the spines, and try to picture whereabouts the novel landed. *You Killed Him.* The title echoes in my head. The accusation.

The lie. I didn't kill him. It was an accident. It wasn't my fault. Who would think that I had killed him? Who would...My mind is swirling, but none of this makes sense. I think that is why I'm starting to believe that it was all a dream. Or a hallucination. Or at least that it wasn't real. Maybe I don't want to believe it. Fuck there's no maybe about it. Of course, I don't want to believe that someone is...what? Fucking with me? Out to get me? What are they even doing? What *were* they doing? It's been a one-off incident. That's all.

The way that my gut is churning as I walk along the bookcase tells me that *that's all* doesn't cover it. I look at the books beneath my fingertips; they are all psychological thrillers. I didn't even realise the library had so many fiction hardbacks in their catalogue. Perhaps the book had come from here after all. Perhaps it fell from the shelf. I'm stretching things here, trying to make up some rationale for what may or may not have happened. I sound like I'm out of my mind. No wonder Fisher wants me to go and see this Doctor Brightside.

I get to the far end of the shelf and stop. I *think* the book stopped here. If it's further down, I'll still see it if I crouch and look below. I just wanted to get to approximately the right place so that the other students on the floor don't think I'm as loopy as Doctor Fisher evidently thinks I am. I bend, trying to make it look like I just dropped something. None of them are looking at me anyway, they are all caught up in their own worlds. I don't think they can even hear me here.

I'm sure it was here.

I turn my head slightly and look under the shelf. There's nothing there. It's a little dusty, but not the thick nasty type of filth that I expected. There's a light layer, like icing sugar on a Victoria sponge. Grey, gross icing sugar. I twist my head quickly, looking along the floor beneath the bookcase. The layer of dust continues, but apart from that there's nothing else in sight.

The book is not here.

I squint at the grey dirt in front of me, trying to work out whether I can see the imprint of where the book landed or not. It's dark and difficult to make out. I couldn't say one hundred per cent either way. Maybe someone shelved it. Maybe. I had counted on it still being here; it would confirm that I didn't imagine everything.

Fuck, I mutter under my breath.

I can't remember the name of the author. I should have paid more attention. All I could think about was that title. The glaring photo of the boy on the cover. But mostly, the title.

I get to my feet and start looking along the books on the shelf. Their names are all very similar.

The Woman Who something.

The Silent something.

Missing something.

The endings of the titles are interchangeable. There's a pattern, a formula. Something about this genre that tells me that the same kind of topics intrigue people. These vague ideas thrill people, I guess.

Secret something.

Lost something.

There are so many of them. I can't see *You Killed Him*. I browse further along the titles. This is hopeless. Okay, what now?

This is a huge library, but the contents are all logged. I can search by title on the library catalogue. I'll find it listed, find out where it's meant to be. I leave the shelf and walk over to the terminal. The screen already shows the search page as a default; I type in the name of the book.

Each letter needles me. The words glare out at me from the screen.

You Killed Him

I look away, towards the keyboard instead,

and hit the enter button.

No entries found for this title.

No entries. No copies of the book. No information about the book. I look at the words again, even though I don't want to see them, but I have to check that I didn't make a typo.

I didn't. I typed the words correctly, even though they are untrue.

It's just a book.

Just a book for fuck's sake.

Just a book.

I run out of the door, and the girl in the hoodie doesn't even flinch as I storm past her. I'm racing so fast down the stairs I nearly stumble. Luckily, my clumsiness kicks in near the bottom of the first flight, and I slam my face into the wall rather than tumbling arse over tit all the way down. That's a Northern saying for you. I'm sure you can work it out. It fucking hurts. I yowl and rub my skin. No blood, but I foresee a black eye in my future. On the bright side (should I tell my doctor about this?) there was no one passing by to see my stupidity.

The accident doesn't slow me. I gallop down to ground and head straight to the enquiry desk.

It's the same woman that I spoke to last time I was here. She has the same vacant, vague expression.

"Can I help you?"

She hasn't even looked up at me. She's writing something on a small cat-shaped Post-it note. She draws a smiley face at the end that bears no resemblance to her own expression and finally, as I haven't spoken yet, she meets my stare.

"What happened to you?" She doesn't mask her shock at my appearance. I must look worse than I imagined. Sleep-deprived, with a battered face and...did I even shower this morning? Have I brushed my hair today? I must have. I had the appointment with Doctor Fisher. That was today, wasn't it?

"I fell," I deadpan. "I need some help finding a book."

I'm sure she sighs before she speaks.

"You can access the library catalogue through the terminals on every floor of the building."

"It's not on the catalogue. In the catalogue. It's not listed." I'm trying to be patient, but I'm tired and stressed and this woman is, for the second time, very unhelpful.

"If it's not listed in the catalogue, we don't hold that title. All books are logged into the computer system. It's how we stop people from taking them walkabout. They are all given a security sticker..." She pulls a book from the pile next to her and opens the back of it to show me. "...and their titles are added to the list so that people can find them. Maybe you typed the name wrong."

"I didn't," I say. "I checked it. Can you look for me?"

"You're asking me if I can I type the words that you typed into the same system and get a different response?" She looks at me like I asked her to gargle frogspawn.

"Please," I say, as though she was making a genuine offer and not just being a sarcastic bitch.

I see her try to maintain her composure and I get a bit of a rise out of it, despite everything.

"What's the name of the author?" Her words are steady, heavy with effort.

"I don't know," I say. "I only know the title."

"Is it for one of your modules? I can look at your reading list if it is."

"No." I don't want to say the words out loud but I'm going to have to. "It's a novel. I think it's a psychological thriller. It had that kind of look, you know? It's called..." I pause and my voice becomes quiet. "'You Killed Him'."

She twitches her lips. "Never heard of it. You *think* it's a psychological thriller? You aren't even sure of that?"

"I haven't read it." I say it like it's obvious. "Can you help me find it?"

She sighs heavily now and starts to tap into the computer.

"We don't have it." She says it in the same way she would say *goodbye*. Like it's the end of the conversation.

"It's not in the library at all?"

She looks back at the monitor and taps some more.

"Are you sure of the title?" she asks.

I nod. The cover is imprinted on my memory. I am certain and I tell her so. She taps away for what feels like an eternity, and then throws me another impatient stare.

"I've had a look on the internet. There's no book of that name. I'm afraid what you're looking for doesn't exist."

My chest thuds and I think for a moment that my heart has stopped dead.

"What?"

"That title isn't listed. Anywhere."

I doubt she has had time to look *everywhere*, she wasn't really searching for an eternity, but I imagine she knows where to look to be fairly sure of her conclusion.

She shrugs. "Someone may have self-published it, and not released it for sale. But it's not listed. Sorry."

"I...I had a copy. I lost it. I'm trying to find another..."

"But you don't know the author?"

I shake my head. This isn't going to get me anywhere. I can see that the woman wants me to move along, and there are three other people in the queue behind me now.

"If you think of any way that you could find a copy for me..."

"Okay," she nods.

I write down my mobile number and then my student email address. She takes it off me and stands the little piece of paper up against the back of her desk. I would bet my kidneys that she's going to throw it away as soon as I've gone. Still, I smile, and I leave.

Chapter Fourteen

I toss it over in my mind all the way back to my room. What does this mean? What does it prove? I have no idea. If I thought that going to the library would help me to put my mind at rest, I was wrong. It's done just the opposite.

I get home, hang up my jacket and drop down my bag.

"No funny shit from you either," I say to my coat. I'm glad there's no one to overhear. The last thing I need is for someone to hear me arguing with my clothing.

My phone starts to ring; I instinctively tug it from my pocket and click the *answer* button, thinking it will be Doctor Fisher with some news about my appointment. The mystery calls I was getting seem to have stopped. I've gone from resolutely not wanting to go back to therapy to being resigned to it to actually wanting to talk to someone. I do want help. I need it.

It's not the health centre on the line, it's my Mum. I grimace, and instantly feel bad about doing so.

"Hi Becky," she says. She sounds genuinely surprised that I picked up. Do I always let it go to voicemail? When was the last time that I actually answered when she called?

"Hi, Mum. You okay?" I smile, so that she can hear it in my voice, even though I'm not feeling at all happy. I don't want her to worry about me. Not any more than she already does, anyway.

"*I'm* okay. How are you?"

I speak before I think.

"The same as I was last time we spoke. It was only a couple of days back." I don't mean the words to come out as they do.

"I'm sorry. I was just watching something on television, and it reminded me of you. I...look I'm sorry, Becky. I don't mean to keep bothering you. It's just...it's hard for me, you being there and just me and Dad here."

I feel like we are going to have this conversation often.

"I know, Mum." I force my voice to soften. I think about her watching her evening quiz shows, drinking her tea, dipping a biscuit into her cup, passing me the pack. I think about Jordan snatching them from me and laughing, while I would race around the house after him. Dad sat in his chair and said nothing; Mum would huff in feigned exasperation and then laugh as we settled back down with her to catch the end of the show. To go from that to be sitting alone in our house, a house that's too big for the two of them alone to rattle around in, well, that must be tough.

"I miss you," I say. And I do. I miss family. I miss home. I miss the past, the way it was before. "It's no problem. Call when you want to." I pause. "And I'll try to remember to call you too."

I hear the smile on her lips.

"Thanks love," she says.

We have little else to say. We speak our goodbyes, I click *end call*, and see that there's a notification of a missed call and a voicemail from the health centre.

The receptionist's voice tells me that an appointment has been made for me with Doctor Brightside for Friday morning, two days from now, and if there's any problem to call them directly. She's left the number as something of an afterthought. The date and time are fine though. I'm just amazed it's so soon. Something about talking to Mum has made me more determined to try. I don't want to go through therapy again, but I need help. I want to be better. I don't know if I mean that in the sense of I want to *get better* and recover from my insomnia, paranoia and all that shit, or if I just want my life to improve. I think that Doctor Brightside can help me, whichever it is.

I hadn't felt that with Balliol.

"I can't help you if you won't talk to me."

It was obvious, but she had to say it.

I sat, staring into space. I fixed my mind on happy memories, ran through some of my favourite days. That's how I got through my sessions with Doctor Balliol.

My first appointment with her had been only three weeks after Jordan died. I hadn't accepted that he had gone, I was nowhere near ready to talk about it.

I didn't realise quite how isolated and alone I was until I didn't have Jordan anymore. I had come to rely upon him completely.

After I lost Mischa, he was my world. He was everything.

Maybe I would have tried to patch things up with Mischa, tried to explain things to her mother, tried to put things right...but I never had the chance.

I arrived at school for my final revision session, two weeks before exams started. I didn't expect there to be a huge turnout, but there were only three other pupils, sitting at the back of the classroom. They were chatting when I walked in, but as soon as they saw me, they were silent. I was used to being talked about, and then I grew used to being ignored. This felt different.

The teacher arrived for the session and couldn't meet my eyes. I tried to concentrate, really I did, but it's pretty off-putting when you think that everyone else in the room is in on something that you're not a part of. It was a low-key class: no jokes, no levity. It felt stifling. I wanted to be out of there, but I knew I had to talk to the teacher. He tried to grab his bag and get to the door before I had a chance to approach him, but I was on my feet and in his path before he could duck out.

"What's going on?"

He didn't say anything. He looked down and pretended there was something really important he had to find in his bag.

I stood my ground.

"What's going on?"

I was prepared to repeat it as many times as I had to until I got a response.

He puffed out an awkward sigh, and got out his phone. I saw him tap out a text message, but still, he didn't speak to me. I didn't see what he typed, but when the reply pinged back, he finally made eye contact.

"Come with me," he said.

He led me along the corridors. There weren't many pupils around, and I was thankful for that. It was crushingly embarrassing following him along, not knowing what everyone else clearly knew. If I had more friends, if I was in the WhatsApp groups and the Messenger chat, if I was Someone You Talked To, the whole hideous walk would have been unnecessary.

I'd lost Mischa. I'd lost her twice. Once when her mother forced us apart and the second time...well, you know the rest. You know what I was told when I got to Mr. Foster's office.

Two months later, I would lose Jordan too.

Chapter Fifteen

Some days I'm too exhausted to do anything. The darkness of night melts into the watercolour grey of day, and I stay in my bed. I get up when I need to. I make some food, take a piss, get a drink, go back to bed. I can go on for so long, just ticking over, but eventually, I crash. I have to take a *Me Day*. I need that time out. If you don't take those days for yourself, I recommend it. Even if you sleep like a baby, be good to yourself. Make time for yourself.

I never really got that saying. Sleep like a baby. As far as I know, babies sleep for four hours, maximum, and spend the rest of their time wailing or feeding. I'd be happy with four hours. I'd be ecstatic.

When the insomnia first started, I used to have to fill in a 'Sleep Journal'. My psychiatrist, Doctor Balliol, asked me to log all the hours (ha!) that I slept, and rate the quality of the sleep. Have you ever thought about the quality of your sleep before? No. You take it for granted. I know. I did too. What is *quality* sleep? Now, it's anything longer than the sharp little snatches that I snap in and out of. An hour feels like a luxury now.

There are a few problems with maintaining

a sleep journal when you're an insomniac. Obviously, I do have the micro-sleeps that keep me alive. For the most part though, I'm not aware of them. Sometimes they are like a long blink, or at least that's how I experience them. If I haven't been aware of the time when I drop off, I'm not even certain how long they have been. I mean, I know I'm not sleeping for like five hours or whatever, but sometimes I couldn't tell you if it's been five seconds or five minutes. It's extremely disorientating.

When I was writing in the journal, I asked my mum to observe me, and to keep the log for me. She couldn't do it all the time, of course. She didn't follow me around all day, she wasn't with me at school. To be honest I was only ever at school or at home after Jordan died.

I didn't have Jordan.

I didn't have Mischa.

I didn't have any reason to leave the house apart from classes.

I thought I was sleeping maybe once or twice a day, for ten, twenty minutes tops. Mum logged two hours' worth of micro-sleeps over a twenty-four-hour period. That's not a lot, granted, but all those little snatches added up to far more than I imagined. I expect that now I probably get four hours minimum over the twenty-four-hour period, but I wouldn't call it sleep.

We heal when we sleep, we grow when we sleep. Our brains need sleep to power down, store memories, get their shit together. No sleep, no chance to do that. This is why I'm so ditsy. I'm literally scatterbrained. My little neurons are trying so hard, but they don't stand a chance.

I spend my free day in my room. Outside it's snowing, and I watch the white haze flicker for a while. It has the same quality as watching a television detuned to static. It's strangely calming. It looks so cold outdoors. I'm happy to be here, in my sweatpants, in my bed. Out there, everyone is bundled in duffle coats or those big puffa jackets that look like glossy sleeping bags. I enjoy watching them, but I have no desire to be out there.

I read for a while. I used to like fantasy novels, those unicorn and fairy type books; I guess it's escapism. Now that my life hovers in a sleep-deprived dream state I don't need fantasy anymore. I go for thrillers these days. I prefer the edge-of-your-seat stuff. If I don't sleep, I can't have nightmares, right? That's not completely true. I can't concentrate on complex plots and long dramas. Give me something simple and gripping.

Give me the short, sharp shock. I lie on my bed, flicking through the pages, reading about a world that is even more messed up than my own.

At around seven-thirty I go out to the kitchen, and expect to see at least one of the others. The room is empty. There are no dirty plates in the sink; there's no sign that any of them ate here. It looks like I have the flat to myself this evening.

I warm up a can of soup in the microwave, putting minimal effort into my culinary endeavours. In the lounge, I rest my bowl on the arm of the sofa and dip at it half-heartedly with a chunk of ciabatta that I can't be bothered to butter. Simple things make me happy. I aim the remote at the TV and scroll through Netflix without really concentrating. I choose a documentary about animals, and nestle down for the evening. I like being in my own space, only myself to worry about. I'm not good company for others, but I'm plenty for myself. With so many hours to fill, I have to be good at filling them.

Everything is calm. Everything is peaceful. I half-watch television, while I scroll through my phone, losing track of time.

There's a scratching at the door.

It sounds like someone is messing with the lock, trying to jam in a key that doesn't quite fit.

I immediately sit up, snap to attention.

I'm so on edge that I look around me for something to use as a weapon, just in case. I can only see the remote control. It's not going to be much use. I could dart through to the kitchen, pick up a knife. Anything.

Voices in the hall, just mumbled noise. I must have been dozing because I'm disorientated and confused.

What can I do? I've waited too long.

The door bursts open.

My housemates pile into the flat.

"Where were you tonight? I thought you were coming to meet us," Cally says.

Her voice is a drunken slur and I assume the others are out of it too.

"I've been here all night. Alone," I say.

I'm not impressed that my flatmates went out without me. My tone is passive-aggressive, but I don't care.

I put the remote control back down on the arm of the sofa, feeling a little foolish. It would have been a useless defense.

"You could have come if you changed your mind. You knew where we were," Cally says.

I could have guessed that they were in the bar, but I didn't *know*.

"Changed my mind?"

"You said 'not tonight' when I asked you." Cally looks as confused as I feel.

She sits down next to me on the sofa. Her breath smells of gin and tonic, so sweet and sickly.

"I haven't seen you since this afternoon. I'm sure I'd remember if you mentioned drinks."

"I knocked on your door. Around seven. Before we went out. I told you where we were going. You said not tonight." Her voice sounds clear now, she's not messing about.

"You heard me say that?"

"I heard it too," Heidi says. "You must have been half asleep, I guess."

"Uh...seven o'clock?"

Heidi nods. "We wouldn't just go without you." She stands in front of me and leans to give me a big hug. Her chest is soft and warm, I could keep my face in her sweater all night. She smells much better than Cally's booze breath. I'm not sure what her perfume is. Something light and floral. Probably expensive.

I don't think about sexual desires. I don't let myself. Right now though, I can't help but feel something. She's unaware of my thoughts. She pulls back and smiles, and I smile too.

Perhaps they did call for me. Perhaps it was during the blink of a micro-sleep. I shouldn't doubt them. What reason do I have?

Not everyone is out to get me.

Perhaps nobody is.

I look at the two girls, and give them a smile that I feel from the depths of my heart. I want to believe that they could be my friends. I want to believe that I deserve them.

Eamon has collapsed onto the other sofa, looking the worst for wear of the three of them. Sometimes I am glad I don't drink.

"Next time," I say, and I mean it.

Chapter Sixteen

My first appointment with Doctor Brightside is at
ten o'clock on Friday morning. I have to take a bus
to get there. I've barely been off campus since I
moved here; I sometimes forget there's a town just
beyond the university's boundary. I've been to the
supermarket, and we almost went to the cinema
the first week we moved into the flat, but we
ended up in the SU bar instead.

The bus ride isn't a fun experience. The
lulling motion of the vehicle, along with the heat
from the vent that runs along the side, beneath the
seats, would be enough to send most people to
sleep. If it wasn't for the kid in the buggy at the
front screaming for the entire journey, even I might
have snatched a micro-sleep.

I'm so irritable these days. These days being
the past two years of my life. I brought a book with
me to read on the journey but it's impossible. If I
keep coming to these sessions, I'm going to have to
get taxis. I could ask Eamon for a lift, but that
would mean more explaining than I want to do.
Neither Cally nor Heidi have cars and I've not
learned to drive. I don't think I ever will. I wouldn't
trust myself to be a driver, but I don't particularly

like being a passenger. I have to sit in the backseat now, like I'm in a taxi or something.

I'm not going to ask Eamon. Definitely not.

I arrive at the psychiatrist's clinic five minutes ahead of schedule. Despite knowing how much I need to be here, I've been dreading my first session with Doctor Brightside. Now, sitting in the drab waiting room at her practice, I feel something bordering on terror. After everything that has been happening, or perhaps not happening, to me over the past couple of weeks, I have plenty to talk to her about, I just don't want to.

I sit and turn the pages of one of those celebrity gossip magazines that I don't care in the least about. It's full of photos of people I don't know doing things I am not interested in. Still, it's better than thinking about the hour ahead of me. I'm staring at a section devoted to some literary party for an author I've never heard of when my name is called.

I make a show of closing the magazine, returning it carefully to its place on the table, and slowly walk down the corridor to meet Brightside.

The consultation room is cold and clinical compared to the private practice I visited back home. I try to hide the look of disappointment on my face as I enter and shake the hand that's outstretched to me.

"Rebecca, hello. I'm Doctor Brightside. Please. Come in."

She's a tall, sleek woman. The kind of woman that looks like she would never need to seek the help of a psychiatrist. First impressions: doesn't have mental health issues. Of course, her first impression of me is exactly the opposite; that's what I am here for. I smile, and go into the small, bright cell.

The private practice had a consultation room that felt more like a study in a rich person's home. Like the kind of place you'd see in a private detective series, if you watched that sort of television show: dark wooden bookshelves, a sofa made from butter-soft leather that smelt divine, tall windows that let in natural light. Even when I hated the sessions, which was most of the time, the room was welcoming, warm and comfortable. Brightside's room is square, bare and stark. The light is harsh and fluorescent. The chairs do seem to be made of leather though, strangely. They're deep and large, and almost fill the tatty little space.

She gestures for me to sit in the armchair by the window, and she sits nearest to the door. The doctor always takes the seat closest to the exit;

I suppose it's a precaution in case the patient becomes violent, threatening, or tries to trap them in the room. I wouldn't have the energy even if I wanted to do something that dumb.

"We have an hour today, and I'd like to get straight into it, if that's okay?" Her voice is as smooth and slick as her appearance.

I nod and she gives me the standard spiel about confidentiality and information sharing and blah blah blah.

"Doctor Fisher has given me some brief details," she says, settling herself into a comfortable position. "But I want to hear from you. Tell me, in your own words: why are you here?"

I was expecting her to ask me to tell her what happened. I suppose in a way that is what she is asking. She's put the onus on to me of course though, phrasing it like this.

The room is silent apart from the ticking of a clock on the wall behind me. I can't check the time without looking around, but it's visible to her throughout the consultation. I'm not being billed by the hour for this, of course; the good old National Health Service is footing the expenses for my sessions. I'm so grateful, especially since I know how much it cost my parents for the private therapist I used to see. There's big bucks in mental health. Perhaps I'm heading down the wrong career path; perhaps I should have stuck with that childish dream I had of being a psychologist.

I do this. I veer off the track, let my mind wander, think about other things.

Brightside is unhurried, sitting in her soft cream leather armchair, her hands together on her lap. I'm thinking about everything other than what I should be saying. I've looked at her shoes and wondered where she bought them. They are shiny black patent leather with T-bar straps. They look both elegant and businesslike. Professional but pretty. The same goes for her dress. It's a simple dark grey shift, short sleeves, modest neckline. It crosses my mind for a moment that she has chosen these clothes specifically not to draw my attention. She wants to have complete control of her clients' concentration. Details are distracting. To me though, the lack of details is just as bad. The absence of something can be as interesting as its presence. Her clothes are smart and stylish but also entirely dull. Her hair is clipped up. Everything about her seems standard, generic and bland. She's wearing simple hoop earrings, white gold, I think, maybe silver or platinum. I don't know why my first thought went to white gold. She wears a small clear stone on a chain around her neck. I assume it's a diamond. Her nails are well manicured, in a neutral pink tone.

She's looking at me, but she hasn't said anything else. She hasn't tried to hurry me, but she hasn't told me to take my time. I wonder if she is taking stock of me in the same way that I have been appraising her. I suppose it's part of her job to do that, but it is part of my nature. We are at an impasse.

I inhale, and I plan for my words to follow on the outbreath, but they don't. The clock continues to click, and I am mute.

I'm starting to feel the pressure of my own silence, but I don't know where to start. It's a story I have told so many times, but where do I begin now? With the most recent events, or back at the beginning?

I reach up and touch the bruise on my face. No one has even mentioned it. Cally, Heidi, Eamon, they've seen this mark on me, and none of them have said a word. I never considered how strange that was until now. Maybe they were embarrassed for me. Cally knows what a clumsy idiot I am. I can just imagine them there in the bar discussing me. My face has started to throb, even though the bruise has been there for days. I don't know. If I told the doctor maybe she'd be able to give me an explanation for why that is. Perhaps I'm just conscious of it; I feel scrutinized, I feel judged. If she could read my mind, what would Brightside make of my thoughts?

Tick, tick, tick, and still, I don't speak.

The doctor looks so relaxed. She's so comfortable with the silence.

"I didn't kill my brother."

I don't know where the words came from, but that is what I say.

There's no sign that she's shocked by my opening line. She pauses, allowing me to continue.

I gulp softly.

"I'm sorry," I say. "I don't know why…" I want to rewind and start again. "I've had trouble with insomnia for the last two years. Since…my brother…I saw a psychiatrist before, back in Yorkshire before I came to university. Back in Harborough. Sorry, I'm not sure how much you already know."

"Carry on, it's fine. I'm interested in what you have to tell me."

She looks absorbed by my words, and it's certainly her job to be attentive to what I say and how I say it. I'm always so self-conscious. I know that everything I do or say is being judged.

I tell Doctor Brightside about the library, the books, the specific book. I tell her about thinking the bag and coat were a person in my room, the girl in the café, the phone calls, hearing my name in the bar. It seems like I am telling the story backwards, or skipping from one scene to the next, out of order. I suppose we tell doctors our symptoms and hope that they will cure us of whatever has caused them.

Brightside nods and makes encouraging noises. She lets me speak until I've told her everything that's happened since I moved here. Of course, that's just the start. Beneath the surface is everything else, everything from before. It's like I've invited her into my garden and shown her the weeds that are growing there, eating into my life, but we haven't gotten started on the root system, and it's pretty fucking extensive. It's beneath the garden, beneath the house, pushing my whole world off-kilter. If she is going to help me, I need to talk about the things that I don't want to talk about. I learned that from my time with Doctor Balliol. Not that she stopped my sleeplessness. Not that she "cured me". We started to work through stuff though. "Stuff" being "my issues".

I can't shake the knowledge that everything that I do is being watched, everything that I say is being analysed. The more I try to sit naturally, and keep my voice neutral, not give too much of myself away, the more I feel that I'm revealing. I would be terrible at poker. My hands are trembling, my mouth is arid. I want to get out of here.

"Tell me about your flatmates."

I'm relieved about the change in direction. Perhaps she can see that I am not ready to go into all of the background detail yet. I wonder how many people she's dealt with, and how fucked-up they were. I always have to compare myself with someone. I wonder if I am the worst, but I expect there are people with far more serious issues than thinking that their clothing is a person in their room.

"There are four of us. Two other girls, one boy, and me. All undergrads, just started like I have."

I don't know what to say. Maybe she just wanted me to talk about something I'd find easier to discuss. I oblige.

"Cally's in the room next to me, she's a Northerner like I am." I smile as I say it. My fondness for Cally clearly on display, I immediately feel self-conscious again. "Then there's Heidi and Eamon on the other side of the flat. I got lucky with flatmates really. They're a laugh and they're clean and tidy." I shrug. "And they tolerate me waking them up at stupid o'clock…"

Brightside smiles slightly.

"Have you spoken to them about your insomnia? Or about anything else?"

"I don't really talk to anyone about everything that happened." I'm used to telling professionals this. "I've told Cally about my sleeping issues. Only recently though. It's not one of the first things you say when you're getting to know people, is it?"

She nods softly.

"I'm here to help you, Rebecca. The more that you can engage with me and open up to me and to the process, the more we can achieve. It sounds like you have had a very tough few weeks. The upheaval of moving here, being away from your parents, that in itself is a huge stressor for a lot of people…is this the first time you've lived away from them?"

For some reason I think of the fortnight in Bridlington, the only time I recall that I've ever been apart from my mum and dad. The only time I was apart from Jordan until June 16th, 2018. I wonder if Brightside knows about Bridlington. I suppose she must. I suppose everything must be in my notes. Maybe this session is a test. See what information I will offer voluntarily. She probably doesn't need to hear it from me though. Not about those two weeks.

Brightside's expression is quizzical, but she doesn't ask what I'm thinking about.

"I guess so," I say. Why didn't I just say '*yes*'?

She probably wonders the same thing. I'm overthinking again.

"It is hard being away from them," I say.

"Do you talk to them often? Your parents?"

I sigh and it probably answers her question.

"I have spoken to my mum. She keeps calling, but...I'm a pretty terrible daughter, you know."

Brightside shows no emotion, she waits for me to continue.

"I know she just wants to know that I am okay. Or as close to okay as I can be, I suppose," I say, and wonder if Brightside senses my guilt-feelings. I should try harder with Mum. I know I should.

The doctor's eyes flick to the clock; my time is up for this week.

"An hour already?" I ask. It's felt longer. It always does. Still, I was just about to talk. It takes me a while to warm up.

"I'd like to see you again next week, if that's

possible?" Brightside asks, and she flashes me another radiant, perfect smile.

"Sure," I say.

I've started this so I might as well get on with it. I came here because I want to get better. I have to remind myself of that. I have to keep remembering.

I'm The Girl Who Sees the Shrink again.

I'm sure as hell not going to be telling anyone that though.

Chapter Seventeen

After my session with Brightside, I take a taxi back to campus. The flat is empty. I make a cup of the Yorkshire Tea that Cally bought for me, and take my mug through to my room. I sit up on my bed and take tiny sips of the too-hot drink. It makes me strangely nostalgic. I guess the effect comes from a mix of the taste of the tea and the conversation with the psychiatrist. I've been a bit of a dick to my mum, I recognise that now. Of course she's finding it difficult with me being away from home, she can't keep her eye on me from this far away. I smile to myself, curl my knees up to my chest and hug them tightly. I should try to talk to her properly. Give her some reassurance. It's the least I can do after everything.

I finish the tea and lie on my side, looking into my room, away from the window. It's really quite a depressing little space. I should maybe get some decorations of some sort. Make it more homely. A vase or a poster or anything to make it look more like a bedroom and less like a prison cell. Feng Shui the place up a bit. It's meant to be my home now.

Home home home. Yeah, I should phone

my mum.

I wriggle my hand into my jeans pocket and pull out my phone. Then I take a breath in preparation, and make the call.

"Hey," I say.

"Oh, Becky. Hi." She doesn't try to hide the surprise in her voice. It makes me feel more guilty than I already did.

We have the general preamble of asking each other how we are, and it's not long before she's back on the usual topic.

"I wish you hadn't moved so far away. I worry about you so much. All the time.'

More guilt. I hate it.

"Mum, I'm fine. Really."

"You were just getting somewhere with Doctor Balliol before you left. I think...you could have...she could have helped you."

Her voice is trembling. I can't bear to hear her cry. I want to stop this. I want to hang up, but if I end the call she will still be there, three hundred miles away, crying because of me.

"Actually, I'm seeing someone. I sorted it out as soon as I got here. I should have told you. So, you don't need to worry. I have a psychiatrist." I use the proper, professional word, trying to sound serious and sensible.

Her breathing calms and I swear I can hear a smile in her voice when she replies.

"Oh love, I'm so pleased. That's such good news. I didn't want to push you into it, but I, well, your father and I, we both think it's for the best if you carry on getting some support."

Support. She always calls it *support*, never *help*, certainly never *psychiatric treatment*. She tries to make me feel less weak, less vulnerable, less needy. I know what I am. I'm not right. I'm not all there. So many things have happened over the past couple of weeks that I think I am possibly losing my mind. I want what my mum wants. I want to be better.

"It's been hard being away from you and Dad," I say, echoing what Doctor Brightside suggested. "Most people find it difficult when they move to a new place without their parents for the first time. And with everything before, you know, I'm more susceptible to stress."

"You're not doing anything silly, are you? And you're eating properly?"

I tense up immediately. My body feels as though my organs have been replaced by lead weights. I sink, leaning back on the bed.

"I'm eating, yeah. I'm...look, there's no danger, okay. Please, don't start..."

Interfering is what I want to say. I don't want Mum and Dad checking up on me, keeping track, calling my lecturers, or my GP or Brightside even. I know she can't tell them anything about me or about what we discuss in our sessions, but I worry about what Mum might say to Doctor Brightside. I don't want her to influence how Brightside sees me. I want my psychiatrist to get to know me for who I am, not for whatever my mum might say to her.

"Mum, really. I'm fine."

There's a near-silence from her end of the line. I can just about make out the background noise of her day, the television quiet, but still just about audible. I try to picture her sitting on the brown boucle sofa, in the sitting room of the only real home I had in my life. I know it so well that it's not hard to bring up the detail; the wallpaper with its out-of-date floral border slapped across the middle, the glass fronted heater with its 'real flame' effect. She'll have that on now, low, to keep the room cosy. She wears slippers in the house, pink slip-ons. Maybe she's pushing her right toes down upon the back of the left slipper now, she has a habit of that. I don't know if she's even aware of it. I know all of her habits. I've watched her for so long.

"Thanks for phoning," she says, quietly.

"I..." What? I don't know. I just don't know what to say to her anymore. "It's okay. I love you, Mum."

I tell her what she wants to hear. It's the best that I can do.

When I get off the phone I flop onto my back and think about getting under the duvet. It's gotten colder whilst we've been talking; it's getting dark already. I reach for the curtain and see that it's starting to snow.

Back home the snow falls thick and deep. My parents' home, until a month ago my home, backs out on to open moorland. Every winter, for as long ago as I can remember, we have had snowfall. Twice there has been enough snow to block the unadopted road that leads from the nearest street to the small row of cottages of which ours was the end building. Sometimes the snow would drift against the side of our house, making a deep slope that Jordan and I could run into. It was an instant igloo of sorts; cold but snug, strangely safe. Jordan. Every memory I have seems strung to him.

Here in Wessex, the snow is hanging in the air, hesitant to land. The blackness of the outside world is speckled by the thick heavy flakes. There's a dark beauty to the scene.

We've only just tipped into November; the trees are hanging on to the last of their leaves. I know they are red, yellow, orange, the fiery end of the spectrum, but in the light of the dying day, they are only shadow.

Lying here I am calm, half-hypnotised. The monochrome world is peaceful.

My peace never lasts for long.

At first, I'm not sure.

I think I see something, but as with most things in my life, there is always an element of doubt.

I don't trust myself.

I don't trust my mind.

The more I look, the more certain I become.

There's a figure.

There's someone down there.

Of course, there are people in the outside world, I know that. What's strange about this person is that they are standing beside the trunk of a large tree; maybe it's an oak, I don't know much about that kind of thing. Anyway, that doesn't matter. They have been standing completely still for as long as it's been since I noticed them, and they don't appear to be moving anywhere. Most disturbingly, they are looking straight up at me, staring at me, into my window, into my room.

They are definitely staring at me.

My first thought is *"is this the fucker from the library?"*.

I was almost over that. I had convinced myself that I'd nodded off and imagined it. Almost convinced myself, anyway. Whoever this is, they are leaning against the tree, not even trying to hide, even though they must have seen that I've spotted them. I can't tell if it's a male or female. I can't make out much at all. They're about five foot six, I guess, around my height, and they're wearing the same kind of standard issue student outfit that most of the people here wear: hoodie and jeans. The hood is pulled up, and I can't see any details of their face. It's not light enough anyway, and they are too far away. It could be anyone.

I scrabble around on my bed to find where I put my phone down after I called Mum. Before I shut my curtains to stop this creep, I'm going to get a photo. I want to have some evidence that this is really happening. I want to have something to take to Security if, well, if this person does anything other than stand outside staring at me. I find the phone tangled in the duvet and quickly turn back to the window.

There's nobody there.

Fuck.

I mean I'm glad this weirdo has moved along but I wanted to commit this to digital memory as well as my own Swiss-cheese consciousness. The snow isn't settling yet, so I can't exactly run down and check for footprints like Nancy fucking Drew. I've nothing to go on.

I hate my stupid, broken brain.

I yank the curtains closed, shut my eyes, and sob.

Chapter Eighteen

After lectures the following day, I'm exhausted. I keep thinking about that figure out there.

All these little fragments, these scraps of paranoia, they are adding up, piling on top of each other. I'll talk to Brightside about them, next session. I'll talk. I will. She will understand, or at least she will help *me* to understand what's going on, or not going on. Everything is such a muddle. I feel like my brain is one of those maps you see in detective films, with the photographs and snippets of information all posted up there, connected by strings. Except I'm missing the strings. My memories, my thoughts, everything; it all feels disjointed, fragmented.

I need to sleep. I've lost sight of that goal, given up on the hope that I will actually ever be able to sleep again. I'm dealing with existing without it.

Acceptance. Surrender.

I shudder into consciousness. Cally is leaning over me, her hands on my upper arms. She's grasping me, and I almost thrash out at her. I manage to get a grip on what's happening in time to stop myself.

I'm in the lounge, on the sofa. I don't even remember lying down here.

"Hey. It's okay. You're okay."

"Fuck. What happened?" I say.

"You must have been having a bad dream. I know you said not to wake you, but you were screaming. Well, yelling." She sits down on the floor next to me and rests her hand on my arm. I don't mind; it feels comforting, grounding maybe.

I shake my head.

"I'm sorry. I didn't mean...I mean I can't help it I suppose."

"Don't be sorry. It's fine, really."

"The others. Are they still out?"

She nods. "Yeah, they aren't back yet."

"I don't really want them to know about..." I trail off. She knows what I mean, as she nods again.

"Of course. Becky, you don't have to say anything but..."

"What? What is it?"

"You kept saying...you were throwing your arms about and...it was like you were fighting someone off."

"Weird," I say. "I don't really remember what I was dreaming." I didn't even know I was asleep.

Without warning, she asks, "What

happened in Chester?"

I feel as though I've been punched in the stomach. I can hardly speak.

Finally, I stutter out the word, "W-what?"

"Chester," she repeats. "When you were thrashing, that's what you kept saying. 'Chester'."

I laugh. I don't know why. It's really not funny. There's nothing funny about it.

"I've never been to Chester," I say, honestly.

She lets out a small laugh too, but it sounds false, forced.

"Funny how our brains work, innit?"

I've been lying in an awkward position that has left me with an ache in my neck. I rub at it as I sit up. Cally scrambles up and onto the sofa by my side.

My heart is still thundering in my chest. I honestly don't remember the dream I was having; Cally seems to know more about it than I do.

I'm relieved when she changes the subject and asks, "Have you eaten? Shall we go get some food?"

If I say yes, we can get out of here, but more than that, I won't have to talk about Chester.

There's the SU bar, *Rachel's* or the *Café on First*, which, as the name suggests, is on the first floor of the shared services building.

"SU?" I suggest.

I've been to *Rachel's Coffee Shop* too many times this week. There isn't much choice on campus though. It's such a closed community.

Cally shrugs. "Sure." She looks at me. "You sure you're okay?"

"Yeah. Just a bad dream, I guess. Lemme just use the bathroom and I'll be ready."

She makes a kooky salute signal with two fingers and grins.

We link arms as we cross campus to the student union building. At least she links arms with me, and I don't resist because being closer is warmer, and it's fucking freezing now. I'm wearing my hoodie, bobble hat, and the thick sheepskin gloves I picked up in a charity shop, and still I'm shivering. I pick up my pace, and Cally steps in time.

It's only half-past four, too early for the night drinkers, but the SU has already started to fill up. The food here is the basic fast food menu: deep fried or microwaved. I go for the chicken bites and cheesy chips: the epitome of beige.

"How are you settling in?" I ask her, between mouthfuls.

I'm aware that in most of our recent

conversations, the subject has been me. My problems, my issues, my past. I want to redress the balance, but also, I'm pretty sick of talking about everything. I definitely don't want her to ask about Chester again.

She shrugs. "Alright." She picks up one of her chips and nibbles on it. "I miss my mum and I really miss my sister, but apart from that..." She flicks her eyes up at me. Maybe she feels awkward talking about her sibling. I have that effect on people; I make them feel awkward.

I nod.

"And your friends? Where did they go off to?"

"All over the place. My best mate is in Aberdeen. Couldn't be much further away! I thought I might get a cheapo flight up there in reading week. What about you?"

I swallow a lump of chickenchipmush that I haven't chewed well enough, and start to cough.

Cally holds out my Coke towards me and I take a gulp.

"Thanks. Um, I don't really have that many friends."

I expect to see sympathy in her expression, but she smiles.

"You have us now," she says. Us. She

includes Heidi and Eamon. I think I might have preferred to have said *you have me*. I could be sure of that. I could believe her. I smile back though.

"How long's it take? To fly?" I'm not that interested, but I want to make conversation. I want to keep focused upon her.

"I didn't look into it really. I just saw that you can fly direct from Wessex to Aberdeen, and thought it sounded fun. I've never flown before. Maybe I'll hate it..."

Behind her, something catches my eye. A girl, on her own. Nothing strange about that, sure, but she's looking straight at me. Now that I've noticed her, now that I'm looking back, she doesn't turn away, she keeps staring.

I think back to *Rachel's*, to...what was the girl called, I can't even remember. Lee's friend. I was about to make an idiot of myself then. I can't do that again.

Cally is still talking. Something about plane crashes. I turn my attention back to Cally and try to ignore the girl behind her.

"Bird strike," she says.

"Bird strike?"

"Like, when a plane is in the air and..." She moves her hands in a way that recreates an explosion. Up and out. "Whoosh. They get caught up in the engine and that's it. The plane is screwed."

I can't imagine how something as small as insignificant as a bird could cause something as large and solid as an aeroplane to just stop working and fall from the sky.

I flash my eyes onto the girl behind Cally. She's still looking straight at me.

Really, Becky. Not this again. Be cool. Stop looking. Stop it.

"Mustn't happen often though. I'm sure you'll be fine."

Bad things don't happen to good people. That's what they say, isn't it? But they do, they do. You can reel off lists of statistics to me, give me the maths, show me your working, tell me the odds, but I know that even if there's a one in a million chance of something happening to you, it can still happen.

What do you think the lifetime (*ha*) odds are of being killed in a car accident? A million to one? A thousand to one? I looked it up, of course. It's two hundred and forty to one. Two hundred and forty. There's about that many people in this bar, maybe a few more. One of them will end up the same way as Jordan. It could be me. It could be Cally.

It could be that girl who keeps on staring.

In America, it's one in eighty-two, so I guess that's a positive to hold onto. You have less chance of dying in an air crash, bird strikes allowing.

Chance. That's all it comes down to? Chance? Of course, it's not just that. Of course not. Things happen. A deer crosses the road. You get distracted. You're travelling too fast. Your drunk sister gets in the way. So many variables.

"Hey," Cally says. "Not going to sleep again, are you? Your eyes were open but…"

"No, sorry." I laugh and dig back into my chicken.

I looked all those things up: the facts, the statistics, the numbers. When the insomnia first hit, and I had all that fresh new time on my hands, I would sit for hours, reading through pages on the internet. One Google search led to another and I fell into a rabbit hole of data. The more I read the more I wanted to read. Next thing you know you're on a website for survivors of RTAs – road traffic accidents – who lost someone in the crash. All these sad, sorrowful souls looking for the kind of answers that the statistics and the numbers can't ever provide.

Just like me.

Those sites, because yes, there are several,

are swimming in guilt complexes. *Survivor guilt*. I diagnosed myself with that before Balliol pushed her glasses up her nose and introduced me to the phrase as though it was a new friend that would be staying with me for a while. That part was true. It's staying with me.

"You could come with me if you wanted," Cally says.

"To Aberdeen?"

She nods. "Yeah. Amelia wouldn't mind. I mean, she'd probably like...she *would* like you. I'll let you know when I'm booking and...you know. Come if you like?"

Cally is so sweet. So unbelievably sweet. Maybe I will go. Maybe it would be good to get away from here for a while. Shit, I only just got here. I've been here almost a month and I'm already thinking like this. Always running. I can't run away from myself. I can't run away from what's inside my head.

When I look behind Cally for the third time, and the girl is still staring at me, I nod at Cally.

"I think that girl is staring at me."

"What? Who?"

"Don't look round," I say, as she looks around. I should have said that first.

She looks back at me.

"The one on that table there? On her own?"

I nod.

"Probably just the way she's sitting. She can't look anywhere else, really."

"Yeah, but…straight at me?"

She shrugs. "Do you know her?"

I shake my head. "Nope."

"Why would she stare at you then?"

"Ugh," I sigh. "I know it sounds crazy, but…maybe I'm just being paranoid."

I look over again. She's still staring. I can't shake it off.

"Maybe," Cally agrees.

A prickle of irritation needles me. I don't want her agreement; I want her reassurance.

I almost open my mouth to tell Cally about the library, but telling her about the library means that I'll start a spiral leading to me telling her about a lot of other things. I can't talk about the library without talking about the words on the computer screen, the note, and more importantly, at least to me, the fact that I'm seeing Brightside.

Being normal and fitting in ranks above discussing my paranoia and my psychiatric therapy.

I don't want to be singled out.

I don't want to be bullied again.

Please. Not again.

Just let me be normal.

Let me get on with my life.

What would a normal person do?

"I'll go and talk to her," I say as though that is the most normal thing I could do.

"I'm not sure that-"

Cally starts to talk, and I know what the next words will be, so I ignore them. I get to my feet and I keep walking.

As I approach the girl, she stands up too. I misstep, a little skip in my track, and I almost decide to stop. I want to speak to her, to ask why she's staring at me. That's the normal thing to do, isn't it?

I hate this kind of confrontation, the type where I don't know what's happening, where someone is getting up, walking...

She's walking away, heading for the door. She must have been staring at me. She must have been. If she wasn't, she would have no reason to leave now. Why would she see me, and then get up and go? It makes no sense.

She weaves between the long tables and mismatched chairs that give the bar its Bohemian ambiance. There are lots of people milling around now, but not enough to conceal her in a crowd. My eyes are firmly fixed on her as I follow.

"Becky!" I hear Cally trying to get my attention again, but I stride purposefully after the girl.

I don't even look back.

If she's the one that's been stalking me...because surely that's what it is, *stalking*, what else would you define it as? If that was her, then I want to know why, and I want it to stop now.

I couldn't see her face clearly enough up in the bar to know if I recognise her. She's another of those hoodie-wearing standard-issue students. I'm not judging, I am one of them too. It's comfortable and easy. I choose my wardrobe carefully to be the same as everyone else. I want to look like them, I want to be like them. I want to fit in, that's all I want.

She could be someone off my course, out of my class, one of the quiet ones that sits in the middle, trying not to attract attention. Would I have noticed her? Would I know her? I can't help thinking about what happened in *Rachel's*. That girl, the last time I let my thoughts get the better of me.

Is that what I'm doing? Is that what this is? I'm second-guessing myself.

I'm still walking. Faster now. Faster because the girl is moving faster.

There's an area between the bar and the exit to the square where the nerdy kids play pool and retro arcade games. We are all nerdy kids here, or at least nearly all of us are. She hasn't looked over her shoulder, not once has she turned to see me following, but she knows. Just how I felt her eyes upon me in the bar, she must feel the burn of my observation, and be aware of my pursuit. She must, because as she weaves between the straggle of overheated teenagers in the lobby, she's almost breaking into a run.

I think about calling out to her, but not here. Not with all these people around. What would I shout? I don't know her name.

Don't draw any more attention than you have to. My brain starts an internal monologue, telling me what to do, what not to do.

The girl pushes the glass double doors open, her hand making a clear print on the steam-fogged pane.

I'm not far behind her. As I burst into the square the cold air nips at my face in tiny little bites, like a cloud of insects.

It's still early. It must be half five at the latest, but the light is dimming.

I think for a moment that I've lost her. There are more people out here, passing through the square on their way back from the lecture block to their dorms, and out from their dorms to the SU. There's a criss-cross of activity; all these bodies, all wanting to be somewhere.

I can't see her. Or rather I can see so many people that could be her, she's camouflaged here. We, in our uniforms, striving to sink into the background, we hide her, just as we hide ourselves. We hide our individuality and our personalities. She and I are both anonymous and unknown. Isn't that what I wanted? To blend in. I keep saying it. Perhaps it's what she wants to. If it is, then she's doing a great job of it right now.

I'm whipping my head from left to right, scanning the crowded square. Over there, by the front of shared services. That could be her.

The dying day has turned everything monochrome. Her hoodie is a colour that I could only faithfully describe as *dark*. If you asked me to be more specific, I couldn't. Maybe the person I'm looking at is taller than the girl in the bar? I'm not sure it's her.

I look back the other way. Down, through the square, the way I would walk home. I see another girl who could also be my stalker, if that's what I'm calling her now. I guess I am.

I'm about to head after her, when a flash of

movement catches my eye.

Going up the path towards the library.

There's no doubt in my mind that it's her. Same height, same build, same clothes. Surely her hoodie is blue? She doesn't have a bag, that makes her standout here amongst the students with their backpacks. Okay, so I haven't got mine with me either, but I was with my friend in the bar. She was on her own. I'm clutching at straws, trying to make sense of my thoughts.

I don't have time to create a life for this girl in my mind. I can't stand here wondering why she does or doesn't have a bag. I have to get after her.

"Becky!"

I must have been standing still for too long, because Cally has made her way from our table to this cold outdoor world. She taps on my arm.

"Becky, what are you doing?"

I look around, give Cally my attention and there, in that split second, the girl slips away. When I look back to where she was, without even answering Cally, there's only an empty space.

There's another short moment where I have to make a decision: run to where the girl was, look for her, track her, hunt her, find her – or turn back to Cally.

"What...Becky. Look at me. What are you

doing?"

Her voice is so flat, so calm. I feel like an animal that she's trying to tame. She's cautious, maybe even fearful of what I might do. This isn't good.

I slump my shoulders, stand down.

I look one more time over at the place where the girl isn't. There's a lot of empty space out past the library. Soon that empty space will be dark empty space, the kind I don't want to be stumbling around in on my own.

I don't want to let this go. I don't want to miss an opportunity to get hold of this bitch and find out what the fuck is happening. But I don't want Cally to think I'm - what? Paranoid? She already does, as far as I can see. Crazy then? I don't want that. That's the last thing I want.

I huff out a sigh that puffs a cloud of frosty white into the icy air.

"I'm sorry," I say. "I've had a really tough week. Overtired, you know. This fucking lack of sleep."

She nods, but I'm sure I see something in her eyes. A sign that she's not quite sure of me anymore.

Fuck. Fuck this. Fuck all of it.

Then I remember. Chester. Why the fuck

was I dreaming about Chester?

Chapter Nineteen

There's no point going back to the bar. I'd pretty much finished my food, but even if I hadn't, I've no appetite now.

I'm not sure that I want to sit opposite Cally facing her questions and judgement either. Still, when we get back to the flat, that's exactly what happens.

I try to turn off into the corridor back to my room, but she puts an arm out and stops me.

"You want to talk about it?" she says.

No.

I can't say it though.

"I don't know what to say."

At least I'm being honest.

"Come on, let's have a brew and you can say as much or as little as you want."

I hold back the urge to roll my eyes.

"Okay. Let me just…"

I want to make an excuse to go back to my room, but I can't think quickly enough. My stupid cotton wool brain again.

I sit uncomfortably in the living room while she busies about in the kitchen making the drinks. I feel like I'm in a waiting room, and in a way I am.

There is this sense of discomfort I get

whenever I have an appointment. Anxiety. Apprehension. I hate it. The waiting is probably worse than the actual sessions. All the things that my therapist, Doctor, parent, friend, whoever's turn it is to interrogate me, everything they might want to ask me, the thoughts jab into me. It feels like I'm being hit by little ninja throwing stars, one after the other, a constant sharp, painful bombardment. Bang, bang, bang, all those thoughts; they overwhelm me. My anxiety stacks thought upon thought, blow upon blow, and I imagine the worst will happen, always.

Of course, I can choose what I want to say, where I want to start the story, what story I want to tell. That's my defence. Whatever terrible thoughts are going through my mind, I don't need to reveal them, I don't need to share everything with anybody. No one really needs to hear the truth.

Cally hands me my mug and sits on the other sofa. She's not too close, but close enough for me to feel uncomfortable. We have sat like this so many times over the past few weeks, and I have never felt like this before. It feels too intimate. I feel threatened, exposed.

"Heidi and Eamon not in?" I ask.

"Couldn't hear anything." She shrugs and

leans in, waiting for me to talk.

At least the therapists always start with a question. My doctor opens with a welcome, asks me how I am. My parents, well, I guess they gave up trying to make me talk. It's so long ago since Mum tried that I don't remember. Cally waits. She drinks some of her tea and then pulls back sharply, blows gently on the surface.

"Look, I'm sorry," I say. This is one way to start. "Was that…I mean…did it look a little nuts?"

"You know what?" she says. "I don't know. I don't really know what you've been through. I don't know what happened. I don't know what's going on in your head."

I stare into my mug. I don't want her to know.

"It's the insomnia. I can't explain. It does things to my head." And then quickly I add, "I'm not mental or anything. Just really tired. Drained. Exhausted."

"What were you going to do if you caught up with that girl?"

I hadn't thought too much about it. Talk I suppose. What did Cally *think* I was going to do?

"I'm definitely not dangerous, if that's what you mean."

She doesn't say anything. She drinks a tiny

sip of her tea and we sit, avoiding eye contact, in silence.

"I never said..." She begins to speak, but doesn't complete the sentence; she doesn't need to.

"I know, but you think it, don't you?"

"Are you seeing someone, for your insomnia?" She means a psychiatrist, I'm sure. I'm not talking about that. No way.

"I've been to the health centre, yeah. I have some meds, but, well, nothing really helps."

Have I had this conversation with her before? It feels familiar. Maybe because I have this conversation with so many people, so many times. There are so many varieties of the truth. What do I want to reveal? What do I want to hide? What do I want you to think of me?

Fuck I just want to fit in. That's all. Don't judge me. Accept me. This is how I am; this is who I am. I'm a mess and I can only ever hide it for so long.

Cally keeps talking.

"I'm only saying, because I worry about you. I'm worried about you. I can see how..." She searches for a word that's inoffensive, but fitting. "I can see how *difficult* it might be for you. With everything. But make sure you're getting the right help."

"And what is that?" I ask, a bitter edge creeping into my voice.

She picks up on it instantly. "No need to be defensive," she says. "I'm trying to be your friend."

What am I doing? Why can't I just be like everyone else?

I feel like someone is watching me. I think someone is stalking me. Someone is fucking with me. It's scary, it's terrifying, but I can't tell you because – if you don't already think I'm crazy, you will if I tell you.

I think this and I don't say it.

Instead I say, "Thank you. Thank you for trying."

There's another short silence, and then I add, "Maybe it will get better. When I settle in. Maybe. It might take a while. Stress, sleeplessness. I'm a mess."

"We all are, aren't we? All of us little snowflakes. All fucked-up in our own ways."

I give a slow, somber nod. It's true. Even if I am a mess, even if I do some stupid things, I can just about blend in with the crowd of other messes. They may not have been through what I have, seen what I have seen or done what I have done, but life can be fucking tough.

So, I say nothing about the library. I don't want to talk any more about how I keep feeling that people are watching me. She's seen me in action; she's seen enough.

Guilt complex.

Paranoia.

Sleeplessness.

Fucked-up.

I know what I am. That doesn't mean I have to tell everybody else.

When I was back home in Harborough, telling people about my insomnia was never an issue. There was no one to tell. I never had to explain myself to strangers. My parents knew, of course, and they were the only people that I really spoke to. There was a meeting with the school, where I sat quietly whilst my parents explained my *condition*, and asked what *adjustments* could be made for me. I didn't want any. I didn't think I needed any.

After Jordan's death I was more motivated than I ever had been before. I had something to prove. I had something to achieve. It was his dream, sure, but he couldn't make it a reality anymore, so I was going to do it for him. I am doing it. I may have lost concentration, but I have gained focus. I know what I am aiming for; it gives me a reason to live.

The teachers were okay. I mean they made predictable quips about me staying awake in class and said that if I needed to sleep during the day, I could go to the first aid room and use the couch in there. I did it once, just to see what it was like. It was predictably clinical. Cold, plastic-covered foam; not anywhere that anyone would ever choose to sleep. The couch was also about three feet off the floor, raised on grubby metal legs; I would probably have rolled off onto the floor if I'd managed the slightest shred of sleep.

Despite not wanting to use the wonderful sleep facilities provided, I liked that there was somewhere that I could go and be alone, if I ever needed to. I did. Sometimes I did. Being around people all the time can get too much for me. It did then, and it does now. Even sitting with Cally, even though it's just the two of us here, I feel a sense of overcrowding.

So, that was school. My parents, well, they had plenty to deal with trying to come to terms with the death of their favourite child. I would say that they wanted me to get back to how I was before Jordan's death, but I think they really wanted me to be the person I was before I became a teenager. Something flipped inside me when I turned thirteen, apparently, and I transformed from that sweet, lovely little princess to become a devil child. I don't think it was my *age* that did it. Probably my hormones. I started my periods and turned into a fucking mental case.

Of course I didn't.

I was just a girl, becoming a woman.

That's all.

And now what am I? I don't know. I don't know who, or what, I am anymore. Some kind of zombie maybe.

Now I'm at uni, I inhabit the land of the living. I'm around people all the time. I have so much contact with others that perhaps I must start talking to some of them. Maybe I have to start explaining myself, my condition, and what it does to me.

Talking about myself means labelling myself though.

It means that other people will label me.

Chapter Twenty

The nights get longer, the days get colder. Bed becomes a more comforting, secure place during the winter months. I don't feel like I'm missing out on anything as I do sometimes during the summer. After I finally persuaded Cally that I am doing my best to be a regular human I spent a few hours binge-watching Chase MD with her before I came back to my room and crashed. I plugged in my earphones, listened to a podcast and floated in and out of my beloved micro-sleeps.

I've been dozing for what must be a couple of hours, tucked up in my duvet, snug and safe, when I suddenly jolt to full consciousness. I open my eyes and pull myself clumsily to a sitting position. The room is dark, but it's not as dark as it should be.

Along the edge of my bookshelf, in front of the neat selection of paperbacks, is a carefully positioned line of tealights, all of them lit.

I frown, trying my best to remember if I did this. I don't even recall buying candles. It's just not me. I pull myself up and stand in front of the shelves. The lights haven't been burning for long. The wax has barely melted on the ones nearest to the door.

I check the time on my alarm clock. Two-twenty. What time was it last time I looked? I came into my room around midnight, I'm almost certain.

Did I do this? I must have done; it's not like anyone else can get in here. My room has a lock, the flat has a lock. Even the block requires a code for security access.

What am I thinking? I'm shaking now. I feel like shit. My head is swimming. Everything is hazy, like I'm seeing it through the shimmer of hot air above a fire.

Fire.

Fuck, I could have burned the room down. I could have set fire to the dorm.

Did I really do this? Candles? Me? I shake my head.

I flick on the light and blow onto all the little flames, putting them out. The bitter aroma of extinguished wicks floods the room. That stench of burning turns my stomach; I think I might vomit. It reminds me of things I don't want to think about. That night. The car, the accident, Jordan. The smell, oh I can't, I can't think about it. I wave my hand through the air, trying to dissipate the odour.

I would never have been this stupid. I can't believe that I did this. I can't believe I would do this. It doesn't make sense.

I can't stay here. I need to get out, but also, I need to work out what the fuck is going on. I grab my keys from the table and head out of the door, into the flat. The corridors are always lit, no matter whether anyone is up and awake or not. I press my ear to Cally's door as I pass. I'm trying to be quiet, in case she is asleep, but I almost want to wake her. I want company. I want to talk to someone about this, someone who will reason with me and tell me that of course I did it, that there's no other reasonable reason.

In the middle of the flat, our shared lounge area is also permanently illuminated, and it's empty. There's no one in the kitchen, no one around at all. I wonder whether I should go and listen outside Heidi and Eamon's doors too, and I pause, trying to decide. Whilst I wouldn't mind waking Cally, and she wouldn't mind me waking her, it's different with these two. They don't know about my insomnia. They don't know me as well as Cally does, not that she really knows me, not really. What would I say to them anyway? This thought helps me to make up my mind.

I go back through the lounge and put my hand on the flat's entry door to pull it open. It moves towards me much too easily; I don't have to turn the catch on the lock.

It's already open.

"What the fuck?" I mutter.

I squint my eyes, looking closely. It doesn't look like it's been forced. It's not broken at all; the door isn't damaged. Nothing to see here.

There's a very small landing that leads off to the stairs on one side and to Flat Four directly ahead. I can see from here that their door is closed. I walk over and apply a little gentle pressure anyway, just to make sure. It's definitely shut, locked tightly, just as it should be, just as our flat should have been.

Everything is quiet. I used to think that silence was one of the benefits of being awake at this time of night. I appreciated the stillness, the ability to walk around undisturbed, doing whatever I wanted. Now I'm worried that other people are doing just that. Not simply *other people*, but *someone*. I'm worried that someone is here, sharing the silence.

I lean over the bannister, and look down into the stairwell. It's well lit, but I see nothing.

I skip down the first few stairs, and adrenaline throbs me forward. Then I reconsider and I slow myself. Quietly, steadily, I make my way down the rest of the stairs. I check the doors to the ground floor flats, both shut, locked, secure. I can hear people inside Flat Two, but it's just muffled noise, nothing I can make out.

I take a breath before I step towards the door that leads to the square between the dorm blocks. The door comprises a metal frame, with glass panels to the top and bottom. Through it, I can see North Block, dead ahead, identical to South, like a reflection of my own building.

I'm not sure if I want to find the outer door locked or unlocked. Do I want to be reassured that no one has been in or reassured that someone has? Do I want the truth to be that I'm not doing things that I don't remember? I can't believe I even consider that it might be worse to be out of control than to have someone, who the fuck, I don't know, coming into my room while I am actually sleeping. The irony isn't lost on me. The tiny window of time for which I am asleep. How would someone know to come in at exactly the right moment? It makes no sense.

I put my hand onto the steel door handle. It's shut fast. Locked. I sink to the floor and curl my arms around my knees, trying to control my emotions. It's no good, I can't hold back my tears.

I'm still sitting there five minutes later, looking through the glass at the emptiness. There's nobody about. Between the blocks, in the square, there are four separate soil beds, planted with bushes and shrubs that I don't know the name of. The path runs North to South, East to West, forming a cross between the plots. I scan the bushes for any sign of movement. I don't know what I expect to see. If someone broke into the flats, got into my room and got out again, I doubt they will be waiting around in some shrubbery for me to find them.

I'm losing my mind here. I must have lit those candles myself. It's a coincidence that someone left the flat door unlocked. It must be. If anyone comes past now and sees me down here, they'll start asking questions. I'll have to start giving answers. I'll have to talk about things I don't want to talk about. I drag my sleeve across my eyes, wiping up the messy tears. I pull myself to my feet and lean with my head against the glass of the upper door.

Just as I'm about to turn around and go back upstairs, I see it: the CCTV camera. On the lamppost at each corner of the centre square where the paths meet, there's a camera, pointed directly at the doors of the blocks. I turn around, look up the staircase. There's another camera there too. I am so surprised at myself that I didn't think of this that I choke back a little laugh. I can call Security, or go to the Security Office. I should go anyway, seeing as someone might have been in my room; they'll be able to tell me whether anyone that shouldn't have been in the building has been lurking around. They'll be able to help me answer my questions.

I don't know what I was thinking when I came downstairs. I'm wearing a short-sleeved Pusheen T-shirt with grey sweatpants. I've got my trainers on, so I guess I must have been planning to run after someone, or to run away. It's November, and the outside world of Wessex in the early hours of the morning is freezing. If I stood out there for more than a few minutes I'd have hypothermia to add to my list of issues. I can't go out like this.

Phone them. Just phone them.

Something tells me that the conversation I want to have with Security is one that I should have face-to-face. I recall the librarian and her shitty attitude to me; I want to be able to explain myself better to Security than I think I will be able to in a phone call. I don't want to be fobbed off. Something tells me that they aren't going to take me seriously if I only call. I want to go down there and demand some kind of action. Play the scared, timid girl, all that kind of thing.

If someone was in my room, if that person

is stalking me, wouldn't they have hurt me when they had the chance? They are fucking with me, for sure, but that's where the line appears to be drawn. All the little incidents are adding up, creating a much larger, more intimidating whole.

Where the fuck is *Security* anyway? They must have an office somewhere, someplace they sit at this time of night, drinking coffee, chatting away the hours. I know that it's nowhere that I have ever been, so that rules out a lot of the campus. I'm hopping up the stairs, back to the flat, back to my room as I think of my plan.

First step: get some warm clothes on. A hoodie, a jacket, maybe even my bobble hat. I can log in to the uni website, check where the Security office is.

When I get back to my room, I stop dead in my tracks.

The tealights are all lit again.

Chapter Twenty-One

I had closed the door behind me; I definitely heard it click shut. I know I did, I wouldn't have left it open, not after what happened before, not after finding those candles the first time. The door was locked shut when I got back here, so theoretically I must have locked it when I left. I must have.

Someone has been here again. This time I am certain. What is this shit? Someone is completely fucking with me. But who? And why? I don't know. I don't have any answers. But I need to find some.

I blow out the candles again and then swipe them off the shelf and into the bin. My paranoid brain makes me check that they are all properly extinguished and I'm not going to be starting a paper fire. They're all dead, it's fine. Nothing's fine, of course, but the candles are fine; good for them.

The more I think about it the more certain I am that I never bought tealights.

I pull my hoodie out of the wardrobe and slide it over my head. As I do so, it snags and I'm in the dark for a few seconds longer than I want to be. I don't like this feeling of not being able to see who or what is around me. I feel a rush of panic and tug my sweater down hard and fast. I spin around, checking there's no one here, checking nothing happened when I couldn't see. Everything is as it was before I started to dress. I throw on my jacket and pick up my phone.

It's after three o'clock now. I want to wake Cally. I want to get her to come with me. I want her to tell me that I'm not losing my mind. Maybe she will even know about the candles, about whether I bought them, I don't know. I'm clutching at straws. I leave her though, because if I was a *normal* person I wouldn't want to be woken up at this time. Not that I'm not normal, I'm doing my best to be. Bottom line is I'm not going to knock on Cally's door at this time. I'm sure she's already starting to suspect that I'm unhinged somehow. I don't want to add fuel to that fire.

I click my phone open and go to my web browser. For some reason I'm distracted by a desire to check through my photographs. I want to be sure that no one has been taking photos of me while I'm micro-sleeping. If this was a movie, that's exactly what would have happened. But it's not. This is my life. I fight off the urge, and instead I log into the university web site and search for Security.

Apparently, their office is located at LH3. Where the hell is *LH*? The initials all refer to the blocks in which the rooms are. It's room three somewhere. That doesn't help me. I click back through to the map of the campus. *LH*. I look at all the buildings around Main. None of them has the initials LH. There's a list at the edge of the page, and I read through it.

LH.

Lake House.

The map of the campus shows the lake, out beyond the library block, confusingly referred to as *TH*. The library is named after the region's most famous novelist, Thomas Hardy. It's through Main, past the SU, and further still. I have nothing else to do. I'm not going to be sleeping. I may as well make the walk now.

As I leave my room, I pull the door closed before me decisively, hearing it click locked. I take my phone out of my pocket and take a photograph of the door, secured. I'll know for certain when I come back that I did this. I'll be sure of myself next time.

I take a photograph of the door to the flat too, once I've checked that is locked behind me, and of the door leading out into the square. I didn't make it outside when I came down the first time, but now, as I go out, I take a look at the keypad on the outer door. I tap in the code, check it's working. It is. I tap in a random four-digit number, and it stays locked. Okay then, someone has the code. I think that, and then instantly I think about all the times that someone has entered the building behind me when I've come in, not having to put the code in themselves. People aren't exactly hot on security here.

I look up at the CCTV camera as I leave. It's pointing straight at me. If someone entered, Security would know about it.

Even with my hoodie and jacket, I'm still cold. I pull my hat down to cover my ears and put my hood up. There's a white sparkle of frost on the paths and over the grass. It looks like it's made of glass shards. In the moonlight, the normal can look magical. My breath puffs out in clouds, my lips start to numb. There's a reason that people sleep during these wasteful early morning hours; it's a mini hibernation through a useless time of the day.

If my hands weren't so cold, I'd probably be flicking through my phone now. Instead, I'm hyper-focused on my environment. It's for the best. I can't get away from the thought that if someone has been into my room, twice, they might still be here now. They might follow me. I still don't feel like their motive is to hurt me, but people are unpredictable. I don't know what the fuck this person is doing; I don't know why they are doing it.

I pick up my pace. I don't break into a jog, but I walk more quickly. I'm ready to run if I have to. I start to think that this might not have been a good idea. The path through to Main and beyond is well-lit, but around the lake, it's going to be dark, even with the moonlight to help me see.

I'm already most of the way through Main. I'm a third of the way there, something like that, if the map is accurate and to scale. As I get to the back of the SU, the track before me turns to darkness. There's a shimmer of light from the moon but it barely makes a difference. The night is clear and unclouded, but I don't like this. I don't like it at all.

I take another step forward and almost collapse when I hear someone shout to me.

"Hey!"

There's a brief moment where I feel what rabbits must experience when they are caught in the headlights, the freezing fear that floods them with adrenaline.

Fight or flight. Which will it be?

Right now, I am bricking myself.

I look around, I think the voice came from my left somewhere, towards the side of the lake. I could keep on walking. I could run. I can just about see the Lake House from here. I can get there before he gets to me, maybe. Maybe.

"Hey!" he shouts again.

Fuck.

I see him now, coming towards me. He has a flashlight, he's clicked it on, and he's shining it towards me. He can see me, but the beam directed at my face turns him to shadow, and means that I can make out even less of the person walking in my direction. All I see is the blinding light.

I really am a rabbit in the headlights now.

Run, I tell myself. You're probably telling me to run too. I don't. I can't.

"You okay?" It's a gruff voice, a low voice, but it's not an unfriendly voice.

As he gets closer to me, I see the light glint off his walkie talkie, and then off his name tag.

He's a security guard.

The relief is almost as strong as my panic was.

"I was...I...something happened." I can barely get my words out. "I was coming to find someone, coming to the Security office. I need to talk to someone."

"You shouldn't be out here on your own at this time of night. This lake is dangerous. We don't want to be fishing young girls out of icy water."

I hadn't even thought about the lake. I hadn't even considered it might be dangerous. I wasn't anywhere near it, but okay I can see what he means. I can also see why that is his primary concern. He clearly doesn't expect there to be dangerous intruders on campus, not on his watch.

"Yeah, sorry," I say.

"So. What was it that couldn't wait until morning? Proper morning that is." He has a thick accent, he's a local.

I haven't actually met anyone else who's not migrated into the area to study or teach here since I arrived. It reminds me how far away from home I am.

"Someone was in my room."

Without waiting to hear anymore, he puts a hand on my back and starts to guide me along the path, towards the Lake House. His light shines on the path in front of us, picking up the frost sparkle, like a carpet of diamonds in the darkness. The beauty seems out of place, considering the context.

"Let's get you back to the office, and you can tell us everything."

Chapter Twenty-Two

In the Security team's office, the guard's colleague is sitting in front of an ancient monitor. It's a cube of a thing, probably a relic from the noughties, and it flicks between images every ten seconds or so. The screen shows the inside of the library: empty. Main: empty. The SU bar: three figures, I can't make out if they are male or female, students or staff, standing in a small group outside the door. Neither of the guards appears troubled by them. There's a phone on the desk, a heavy black block. I haven't seen a landline in years. This place could be a museum for antiquated technology. I should have known when I clocked the walkie, hardly hi-tech.

The men themselves look like their style got stuck in a past decade too. I could be in a retro movie from twenty years ago.

Now I see the guy from by the lake in the light of the harsh fluorescence, I'm surprised to find that he is a lot younger than he sounded. He's probably around mid-twenties, not much older than I am. His uniform is too big for him, and he has a haircut that was stylish in the 1990s: centre parting, flat, straight curtains of mud-brown hair stuck to his brow. He's still fighting off his teenage acne. The other guy is older, taller and wider. His uniform is probably the same size as Mr. Britpop's, but he fills it out, his gut pushing at the buttons. Maybe in a few years, Britpop will look like his colleague. Maybe they'll be indistinguishable.

Britpop gets me a mug of tea that I didn't ask for, and we sit down in the cramped room. There are only three chairs, so Britpop perches on the edge of the desk. He towers over me, and I don't like it.

"Tell us what happened, love," the older guy says.

I thought that I had calmed down, but my hand is shaking so heavily that I spill the tea out onto my pants. It's hot, and I jump, splashing out even more.

"It's okay, love." The man reaches across the desk and pulls a few tissues from a box and passes them to me. I mop clumsily at the dark mark on my leg.

"Thanks," I say.

Then I start to tell them everything.

I describe what happened in the library, the figure I saw from my window, and the tealights from tonight. I leave out the phone calls, I don't think there's much they can do about that. I keep to the facts, and try not to cloud the description with my emotions, but I'm shaking and teetering on the brink of tears by the time I'm done.

"Can you help me?" I ask.

"That's quite a lot of information there. Seems like there's been a lot happening."

I nod. "Yeah. There's been a lot. I need it to stop. It's really, *really* getting to me."

They both look at each other and then look back towards me.

"We'll do what we can, love. Of course."

The older man coughs. He sounds like a tractor spluttering to action. He makes big, fat, blubbery sounds to match his big, fat, blubbery figure.

The other guy looks thoughtful like he's trying to come up with something more useful.

"The footage isn't stored here, so we'd have to wait until morning to check that out," he says.

"Jack will go with you to have a look around South though. See if we can find anything suspicious," the big guy adds.

"Any signs of forced entry or loitering..." Jack, formerly known as Britpop, says.

He sounds like he's watched too many detective programmes on television. Maybe that's what they do all night while they are on duty. That, and walk around the lake scaring unsuspecting people.

"The doors didn't look as though they'd been forced though. Like I told you, the door to my flat was open, unlocked."

"Is it possible you left your room unlocked too? Someone could have come in while you were sleeping." The older guy is full of good ideas.

"I don't sleep. I can't sleep." I obviously didn't explain the definition of insomnia clearly enough.

"Maybe this time you were though," he says.

Sure, I think. *Sure. All of a sudden, I can sleep. I'm cured.*

Security Crack Duo: one.

Medical Science: nil.

Maybe I'm asleep now. Maybe this is all a bad dream.

I must have reflected my thoughts in my facial expression, because Fats shakes his head at me and turns away.

Jack stands up and turns his torch on and off, like he's running through some preordained standard drill to check it's working before he leaves the office. It was fully functional twenty minutes ago, and it is now. If I'm dreaming, this part is particularly dull.

"Let's go and have a look," he says, like I'm one of the team now. He heads out of the door, and I follow.

The block is still silent when we return. Too early yet for students to be up and about unless those students happen to be insomniacs, or just plain nuts. Before we get the door, Jack starts to shine his torch around on the floor, aiming the beam at the soil that forms a two-foot border around the building. It looks like there were flowers here once, and maybe there will be again when Spring comes around, but right now it's just hard dirt. I guess he's looking for footprints or for something that has been dropped or discarded. I could imagine someone standing around, waiting for their moment to sneak inside, smoking, dropping a pile of butts, or getting through a few chocolate bars and leaving their wrappers, just so there was evidence of them being here, like a bad plot line in a thriller. There's nothing. I don't think people really do that, unless they want to be caught out. Maybe then, maybe if they want to leave a sign.

We walk right around South and come to a stop by the front entrance.

"Nothing?" I ask.

He's been silent while he does his detective

bit, and I'm not one for unnecessary conversation, as you may have gathered.

"Not yet. The ground's a bit hard for footprints." The snow never stayed, never settled. I don't know if it would have helped. "No signs that anything's been disturbed. Nothing left behind. Not that I can see."

He sounds like he's enjoying this. I guess if I sat in an office with Fats every night, I'd be glad of the chance to get out of there and do some real work too. Who signs up to work for campus security anyway? Whose dream job is that? Someone who wants to be in the police force but can't make the grade, or someone who left the force for a more sedate role, maybe. Jack's too young for the latter, so maybe he tried and failed. I can't see Jack as a copper, somehow, but he's probably made as many assumptions about me as I have about him.

He's started to prod at the edges of the security code panel. I don't know what he's expecting to find there.

"You say you tried the code, and everything looked like it was working out here?"

"Yeah. I tried the correct code and then a random number. The right one opened it. The made-up one didn't," I say.

He makes a humming noise, and then enters the code for the building. I suppose Security must have the codes for every block, but I'm impressed he remembers it so easily.

I'm glad to be inside. The lobby isn't all that warm, but it's much better than the November pre-morning outside. Jack shines his torch around the doorways of the downstairs flats, and then leads the way up to my floor.

I don't even bother to look in the direction of Flat Four across the hall, because I can see immediately that the door to *my* flat is open. Not just a crack, but it's wide open.

I point and Jack nods.

He gestures for me to get behind him, and he semi-crouches, moving forward slowly into the flat. He has flipped his torch to wield it like a weapon. It looks like he has been trained for this, but from his nervous tremor it also looks like he's never had to put his training into action.

The living room is empty. He moves each sofa slightly in turn, looking behind them, as if an intruder would want to squeeze in there between sofa and wall. He waves for me to stand next to the television, in the corner of the room. He must have assessed that it's the safest place, so I do as he says.

He crouch-walks into the kitchen and all I can hear are his footsteps on the cheap linoleum floor. The door creaks open, and he walks through to the corridor between Eamon and Heidi's rooms and the bathroom they share. I realise that although he left me in what he thought was a secure spot, if anyone bursts in from the landing or from my corridor, I'm pretty screwed. I squat as close to the television as I can and try to make myself invisible.

When he creeps back in, he wrinkles his brow as he looks at me, and then holds his hand up in a "stop" sign. He mouths, "Stay there". I don't really want to, but I nod, and I stay.

He goes through into my corridor.

I wait while he looks at whatever he's looking at. My pulse is racing; I feel sick.

He comes back into the living room walking normally, and says, "There's no one there now."

I sigh and stand up, hoping the nausea will pass.

"Do you mind if we take a look in your room?"

"Sure," I say, and I follow him.

As we get to Cally's door, it opens, and she stands with her black bob fluffed up on one side, rubbing her eyes. She immediately sees the security guard, and snaps fully awake.

"What's going on?" Her voice is serious, concerned.

"I'll tell you later," I say. "I'm okay. Sorry we woke you."

I hear noises from behind me and my heart just about stops, but it's only Eamon and Heidi, stumbling from the lounge to find out what the disturbance is.

"Shit. Sorry."

I'm more embarrassed than scared now. My face is burning tomato red.

I unlock my door and push it open. Jack goes in first, and turns on the light. Nothing to see here. My room is exactly as I left it.

"Nothing," he says.

"I thought there was someone in my room," I say to my flatmates, in my most apologetic voice.

"Again?" Cally says, and then bites her lip. "I didn't mean..."

"It's okay," I say. "The flat door was open..."

"I meant to report that," Heidi says. "If you don't pull it tight-closed behind you it's not been shutting properly. I only noticed when..." Whatever she was about to say, she stops herself from saying. I look at her, expectantly.

"I popped over to Four earlier. When I came

back it was open. I pulled it and pushed it, and yeah. It's not shutting properly."

All of our eyes are on her, wondering if she is going to tell us what she was doing making a late-night call to Four. Of course, we already know. There's a hot, really hot, Brummie called Michaela who lives there, and I'm sure something has been brewing between the two of them. Eamon and Cally know it too, from the look they pass between themselves, and then give Heidi. Good for her, at least someone around here is happy.

I don't mention the candles.

"I'll get someone to come and fix the door when the morning crew starts," Jack says.

"And the security tape?" I prompt.

"Yes, we'll have the video checked tomorrow, I mean later today, too. I'll get someone to let you know if there's anything worth seeing."

I nod; Cally puts her arm around me.

"You alright?" she whispers in my ear, and I nod again.

It's half-past four. I don't want to go back in my room alone, but I have to let the other guys go back to bed. I need sleep just as much as they do, but they have far more chance of getting some.

"Thanks again," I say to Jack. He nods and heads off back out of the flat.

Chapter Twenty-Three

I stay in the living room after Cally and the others have made their way back to their rooms, and back to sleep. The more I think about it, the more difficult I find it to believe that someone was in my room. Sure, at the time, seeing those candles, it threw me, but I was half-asleep, half-awake. It's like the whole glass-half-full thing, isn't it? Which am I, if I am only ever mid-way between the two? Either way, I'm not all there. I'm never all there, wherever *there* is. I don't even know that anymore.

I sit on the sofa, letting these thoughts circulate uselessly through my addled brain. It doesn't make sense to me that someone could have been in my room, probably because I can't see why someone would make the effort to break and enter just to create ambient mood lighting for me. I guess I can't know for sure either way. I'd remember lighting the candles the second time though, wouldn't I? I'm not even certain of that. I should have taken a photo of those too; maybe I ought to keep a record of everything I do, so at least I can check back and have some evidence of what the hell I am doing, or not doing. I'm doubting everything now. If you don't know your own mind, if you don't even know what you have or haven't done, what *do* you know? Once you start to doubt yourself, what do you have? Believe me, my life feels like a very fragile existence.

I don't really know what to do with myself. I want to find something to distract me from my thoughts. I feel like this way too often. There are too many hours in the day to fill when you don't spend a third of your life sleeping.

Eventually, I go back to my room, as much for a change of scene as anything. The tealights are still in the bin. I don't know if I thought they would be back on the shelf, glaring at me. I suppose I half-thought it. Half-asleep, half-awake, half-thinking. That's a good summary of my life.

I try to study, I read a book, I masturbate, and then I try to study again. All of these things are equally dull. I don't get much pleasure out of anything anymore. I'm still not willing to own the word *depressed*. I'm stressed, yes. Sleepless, sure. Paranoid, guilty, messed up, yeah, we've heard it all before. Play us a new one. I have four more hours to kill before my lecture, and with only my thoughts for company, they are going to feel even longer.

I get through the day without any incidents. The whole home-décor-loving-intruder thing starts to feel like a distant dream, and I feel like an idiot for how much I over-reacted. That's what it must have been. Okay, so the door to the flat was open, but Heidi said that she knew about that already; it could have been completely unconnected. I was dazed, confused, surely?

But that doesn't make sense.

I have absolutely no recollection of where the candles came from. I don't even *like* tealights; buying them seems so unlike something I would do. I've not left campus since I started here. It's not something that I would impulse buy at the supermarket.

I talk myself around in circles. I swing from being convinced that there was someone there back to complete certainty that the whole charade was caused by my own stupidity and muddled memory. If it wasn't for everything else that has been happening, I might be able to believe that it was all in my mind. The phone calls, the library, the girl in the bar; the tiny drips are pooling together and if I don't get a grip, they are going to drown me.

There had to have been someone there. It's the only explanation. I need to know. I need to be sure.

I'm back in the flat, back in my room, and definitely alone, when my phone starts to ring.

I look at the screen. It's just after three in the afternoon. Apart from the underwhelming hour I spent in my lecture, I've successfully wasted the best part of a day.

It's a local number, not one I recognise, but who really remembers numbers? At least it's not my good friend *Unknown Number*. The laughing girl seems to have found something better to do. She's given up. Even she can't be bothered spending time on me.

I answer the call.

"Becky Braithwaite?" It's a man's voice.

"Yeah? Who is this?"

"My name is Richard Hogan. I'm part of the security team."

I pull myself upright. "Yes," I say. "Did you look at the tapes?"

"I have checked through the footage from the cameras around your block and the other blocks in the square at the times you specified."

"Okay," I say, impatiently.

His voice is robotically neutral.

"There was only one person near the

building. I'll need you to come into the office, but based on the description that Jack left, I believe the person that we captured on camera was probably you."

"What?" I feel like the breath has been sucked out of me. "Are you sure that you looked far enough back on the tapes? You might be wrong. Can you check again? That can't be right. Someone was in my room."

I didn't know how sure my mind was of this until I said the words. They fall from my mouth before I have the chance to think, so they must be true.

"Did you see someone in your room?" He's still emotionless.

My room suddenly feels very cold. I wriggle, trying to get comfortable, but the discomfort is in my mood, not in my body.

"No. Like I explained to Jack and, er, his colleague, I didn't see anyone. I saw, well, I didn't see anything. Someone lit candles in my room. I mean they put the candles in here, and they lit them."

"No one threatened you? No one said anything to you? And you didn't actually, physically see anyone?"

When I had explained everything to Jack

and Fats, I got the feeling that they believed what I was saying. They were reassuring and comforting. This guy is just a dick.

"No."

"Well like I say, you can come down and have a look at the footage, but if I were you, I wouldn't waste any more time."

Great. Very helpful.

"Thanks," I say, and I end the call.

I'm seething after speaking to Hogan. I could go in, and maybe I should go in, but his invitation wasn't particularly inviting. Is it my time that I am wasting or theirs?

Do I really want to be stuffed into that squeeze of a room with this guy who has obviously already made up his mind that nothing untoward happened? I've been through so much, had so many people judging me. Is it even worth doing that again?

Maybe I'm scared that he's right. That I *was* the only person that came in or out. That I lit the candles myself and forgot all about it in confusion. It is possible, after all.

Probable?

I don't know.

I decide to have dinner and think it over.

I don't feel like cooking. You might have noticed that I rarely do. I pull my boots on, and pick my coat off the hook, and leave my room. On the way past, I press my ear to Cally's door. It's silent, but I knock anyway, just in case.

There's no answer, as I expected. Much as I enjoy being alone, I'd quite like some company at the moment, but it's not friendship I'm after, it's a witness. There's been so much crazy shit going on, but only when it's just me, myself and I, never when I'm with someone else. I'm not wishing for anything bad to happen, but if it does, I'd like someone to be with me.

I trot through the lounge and kitchen to the other side of the flat, but Heidi and Eamon's rooms are also empty, or at least there's no answer when I knock.

I'm inexplicably angered by this. There's a weird injustice in the fact that for the first time in a long time I've actually wanted company, and there's none to be had.

Fucksake.

I go over to *Rachel's* for dinner, if a chicken burger and fries count as *dinner*. It's food at least.

The café is packed out; lots of teenagers are too busy to cook for themselves tonight. Sometimes crowds like this make me anxious, but today, being around people makes me feel safe.

"Becky".

I hear my name. The word comes from my left, behind me. Immediately I flash back to the student union bar, that voice saying my name over and over.

There's no one to be seen.

Not this again. Not this.

I almost laugh at how stupid I was, thinking I would be somehow safer in a crowd.

"Becky!"

It's more insistent this time.

I turn my head around, just as there's a tap on my shoulder. I almost collide with Cally's arm as I spin.

"Shit!"

"Sorry," she says, but doesn't smile. "There's a whole shitstorm going on over at South."

"What?" I'm just getting over the fact that it was Cally and not some weirdo stalker that was saying my name, now I have to work out what she's telling me. I cough on the mouthful of burger and put it down.

"I don't know. I've not been over. I was upstairs talking to my tutor and heard someone say something. I'm not sure."

Hearsay then. Great. Nice. Vague.

"Okay..." I say, probably sounding as impressed as I feel.

She looks down at my food, probably assessing how long I'm going to take.

"I'm running back over to see what's going on. You staying to finish that?" She nods towards the sad little dinner.

I hear the siren of an ambulance.

So, there is something happening; now I'm interested.

I take a final bite of my burger, and can't control my curiosity any longer.

"Let's go," I say, and I throw the rest of my meal into the bin.

We see it as soon as we get onto the path. The ambulance is parked on the square between the residential blocks. Its back door is open, and the green-uniformed crew are just visible in the lobby of South. As soon as I know they are indeed in our building, I break into a run. Cally is by my side, keeping pace.

"Who is it? What's happened?" I ask a

student that I don't recognise. They aren't from our block; it's become a spectacle already.

There's a small group gathering, creating a hum of noise.

"Someone's unconscious in the lobby," a girl I've never seen before says. She shrugs and turns back to watch.

"Fell downstairs," someone else helpfully chips in.

"Who?" I ask. I don't wait for a reply though, I push through. "I live here. Move out."

The paramedics are slipping a board beneath the girl in the lobby. I recognise her immediately. It's the redhead from Four, Michaela.

Eamon is on the stairs, watching with a couple of Michaela's flatmates. He's keeping out of the way, but keeping his eye on the action.

I duck behind the paramedics and head up to join him.

They're putting her onto a trolley now. Her eyes are closed, but her face is pink. Her freckles burn like wildfire.

"What happened?" I whisper to Eamon.

"No one saw," he says. "Someone from Two came into the building and saw her at the bottom of the stairs. I guess she fell."

"She'll be okay," I say. "I mean, she looks

like she'll be okay."

As they wheel her to the door, I see Heidi racing down the path towards South. Her hair flaps like a spaniel's ears.

She was walking, arriving on the scene just as I had, but I guess she saw the flash of Michaela's hair glowing like a beacon.

Heidi stops by the head end of the trolley. She's speaking to the paramedic, but I can't hear what she's saying.

I look at Eamon and then head down the stairs to stand at Heidi's side.

I put my arm around her, trying to be supportive, but I don't really know what to say. She leans her head onto my shoulder.

"Will they let you go with her?"

"I didn't even think to ask," she says, and looks back to the paramedic, directing the next words at him. "Could I come?"

"Are you a relative?" He asks the question, even though it seems obvious that the girls are both students and they look nothing alike.

"Friend," she says.

More than friends, I think.

"She's going to be okay, best to call the hospital later, they'll be able to give you some more information."

We watch as they push the trolley into the back of the ambulance and close the doors.

"I only saw her a couple of hours ago. It's crazy seeing her like this, now."

"Hey, they said she will be okay. Don't worry." I reach my hand up and gently stroke her hair. "It's going to be fine."

She smiles bravely.

"Maybe Eamon will take you up to visit her later when she's settled?" I gesture up to the stairs, where he's still standing, chatting to the guys from Four. He sees me, and gives a little half-wave.

"Yeah," she says. "Maybe."

I'm not sure she even realises that I've picked up on what was, or is, going on between her and Michaela. I suppose most people wouldn't notice it, and would assume that they were just friends. I can see those little nuances though. I can read them. Still, I don't mention it. I'll leave it up to her to talk about it if she wants to.

It's strange seeing the ambulance driving off up the path. The only traffic that we ever get on campus are maintenance vehicles, there are no proper roads. The staff and student car parks are way beyond the square I live in, by the three tower blocks that house the students who don't live in

North, South, East or West. Hardly anyone lives in town because it's so expensive here. Landlords don't want students, and students don't want to pay triple the rent that they would in the halls.

"Hey," Heidi nudges me. "Like you said, she's going to be okay."

"Uh, what? Yeah. I'm sure she'll be fine." I smile, and realise I'm still holding onto her. "Let's get inside. It's freezing."

I pull my arm down and link with hers, gently guiding her inside, and up the stairs to our flat.

I get the kettle on and Eamon sits next to Heidi on the sofa. I can hear him using a soft, quiet voice, trying to comfort her.

My hands are shaking as I spoon coffee from the jar, into our mugs. I take a few deep breaths, and run my wrists under the cold tap.

Poor Michaela. Poor Heidi.

Hopefully Eamon will take her to the hospital to visit. He's good at being supportive. I don't think I could bear it. I hate hospitals after everything that's happened. I'm not going to be volunteering to go with them.

Michaela's going to be okay though.

Heidi's mug is shaped like a man's head; he

looks like a Rastafarian. The word 'Jamaica' is printed in a banner across the bottom. I guess it must be a souvenir of a holiday there, or a gift from someone who's been. The furthest I've ever been from home is here.

I take another deep breath and sweep the mug onto the floor.

There's a resounding crack as it smashes into pieces. The broken face of the man grins up at me. His eye is one on shard, his mouth on another.

"Fuck," I say loudly. I pop my head into the lounge area. "I'm so sorry, Heidi. Fuck." I shake my head and walk over to her. "I'm feeling a bit wobbly," I say. "Maybe I shouldn't have offered to make the drinks!"

Eamon starts to stand up.

"It's fine," Heidi says. Her eyes are red; she's dabbing at them with some toilet roll that Eamon has produced from fuck knows where.

"Becky, you sit with Heidi and Cally, I'll sort out the drinks." Eamon heads to the kitchen.

"There's all that mess on the floor now...I..."

He holds out his hand to stop me from talking. "It's fine. You've had a shock, the both of you. Sit tight. I'll sort everything."

I let him go.

Heidi rests her head onto me again.

"I can't believe it!" she says.

Cally sits quietly, making soft, soothing noises. She's not adding anything to the situation.

"Do you..." I don't want to ask this, but I have to. "Do you think this is related to...you know...what happened with my room? I was just wondering if you think someone is...I don't know. I don't know what they are doing. Someone gets in my room, then Michaela falls downstairs."

She looks at me like she hadn't connected the events. Maybe I shouldn't have said anything.

"You don't think it was an accident?" Heidi says, wide-eyed.

"Of course, it could be an accident. I'm just on edge because of before. I'm sure that's all it is. I'm sorry I said anything."

I've not done a good job of calming her, that's for certain. We sit in awkward silence, the three of us, waiting for the distraction of drinks.

Maybe she doesn't even believe that someone was in my room. None of them look concerned. Not about me, anyway. They haven't even asked what happened.

It's a couple of hours before Heidi gets the call from the hospital. Eamon offers to take her up there, as I knew he would. It turns into a flat-evening-out as Cally volunteers to tag along. I don't think she's even spoken to Michaela. Not really. Now all of a sudden, she wants to sit by her bedside and look at her bruises. No, thank you. Not for me.

When Heidi asks if I want to go too, I tell her that I don't like hospitals, and leave it at that. I mean I don't, it's not a lie, but the main reason I don't want to go is that I am not interested in their bandwagon.

They leave the flat, Heidi in the middle and the other two to either side of her. How supportive. What good friends they are.

I can't stand it.

Chapter Twenty-Four

I sit in my room and don't even bother putting the light on. I haven't eaten since the half burger I had at *Rachel's*, but I'm not hungry. Even if I was, the last thing I want is to go back out there tonight. It's cold, it's miserable, and so am I.

Michaela. I mean she seems nice enough. Why would someone push her? Why did I even suggest it? I'm so caught up in my own little world and the mess that I call my life that I am creating drama out of everything. I wouldn't be surprised if none of them want to talk to me again after this. Maybe I'll move out, let Michaela have my room. They'll be much happier with her in their group rather than me. Maybe she can move straight in with Heidi. Why not?

The way Eamon and Heidi looked at me when I said I don't like hospitals, too. They pity me. That's probably the only reason they talk to me. Even though they know nothing. None of them know anything. No one does.

I actually didn't spend long in hospital at all. Back when it happened, I mean. I was only taken as a precaution. To check me over. I still had to lie on one of those body boards, with a neck brace and all that shit. Just a precaution.

They were still cutting Jordan out when they took me. It was his side that took the force of the collision. You don't want to know how many times I've asked myself whether he turned the wheel at the last minute, trying to save me, sacrificing himself. I don't know. I don't honestly know.

I remember the sounds more than anything. Is that weird? We were listening to that song. Our song. *The Testaments*. Our favourite band. The music was loud, blaring from his crappy car stereo. It was midnight, or just before midnight, but we were out of town, down on the backroads. No neighbours to annoy.

Crank it up. Blast it out. Sing along.

That song. I can't listen to it. I couldn't ever listen to it again.

You and me. We're on a path. We're on a roll.

You know the song? You'll have heard it on the radio. It was everywhere that summer. I couldn't fucking get away from it.

You've got me. You've got my heart. You're in control.

We loved it. We loved them. They were our local band that made it big, and we felt like they were our discovery. Our boys, yeah. When they started to get played on the radio it felt so exciting every time we heard them. After the accident, I wished no one had ever bought their music. I wished they'd been a flop, so that I didn't have to hear that fucking song everywhere I went.

You want to hear something funny? When I was in the waiting room for my first psych appointment, that song came on the radio.

Control.

That's what it's called.

'Control'.

I started to feel nauseated every time I heard it. I half-expected the track to stop, exactly where it had when we collided with that tree.

When we skidded off the road.

When the car spun in a full 360, throwing me against the window.

When the driver's side of the car was crushed, compacted, crumpled.

When Jordan's chest collapsed under the pressure of the impact.

When the front end of the car pushed the engine through into where his legs had been, obliterating them, corrugating his body.

When everything changed.

When everything ended.

You and me.

I can hear it now, echoing around my head, as clear as if that radio was in this room.

We're on a path.

Stop it. Just stop it. Stop thinking. Stop.

I hear the song and I can see his face.

Even in those last seconds, when I knew it was hopeless, when I could see he was beyond help, he looked at me. His eyes. Fuck. The way he looked at me. I mean, I know that he had probably already gone, that his mind was probably already gone, but, well, I thought I saw something there. I thought he was sending me a message, trying to tell me to go, to save myself. He wanted me to get out, to escape, to go. He wanted me to be safe. I'm certain it would have been what he wanted, even though he couldn't say it.

We're on a roll.

I need to stop.

I've never had an anxiety attack, not so far, not yet. Still, I can feel my heart pounding; there's a heavy, throbbing banging in my chest. Maybe my blood pressure is spiralling up, out of control. Maybe if I keep lying here, thinking about the things that I shouldn't think about, then something inside me will burst. Maybe.

I do the only thing I can do when I feel like

this.

I phone Mum.

Somehow, she knows, as soon as I start to speak. Maybe I'm less in control of my breathing, maybe I'm rushing over my words. So many maybes.

"What's the matter?" she asks. "What's happened?"

I don't know what to say. I just wanted to hear her voice, to hear something familiar, something from when I was happy, something from *before*. But this isn't before, this is now, and there's no going back.

"I felt like talking," I say. "Tell me about home. Tell me what you've been doing?"

I think it's a simple request, but I don't call very often, and I understand that my sudden interest might have taken her off-guard.

I hear a small creaking sound at her end of the line, and I picture her bending her knees, settling into the sofa. It has a slightly loose spring at the end that she always chooses, closest to the table, where she puts her mug and the TV remote. I try to imagine her there now, what she's wearing, whether she pinned her hair back today. I close my eyes, trying to paint that mental picture.

"Why? What's happened?"

My eyes snap open again. She can't give me what I need, not even this once. Just words, that's all I want, normality. I'm not sure it even exists anymore.

Did it ever?

I sigh.

"Rebecca."

"I'm tired, Mum. Tired and stressed."

"Something in particular?"

"Everything. I…" I'm about to tell her about the phone calls, the library, Michaela, everything, but I stop myself. "It's hard. Being here. Coping."

"Have you seen someone? You said you had a…"

She doesn't finish the sentence. It's as if she doesn't want to mention the psychiatrist, like the word would be a curse of some kind.

I bite my lip.

"A professional, you mean?"

"You know what I mean," she says. I want to hear sympathy in her voice or concern, but all I hear is exasperation.

"Yeah. She seems okay. She hasn't ditched me yet."

Of course my mum knows that there's more chance of me ditching Brightside. It was my choice this time, though, to start the sessions. I wanted help. I moved here to get on with my life and to do the things that Jordan will never be able to.

"Have you spoken to your *doctor* about...well, have you told her everything?" She pauses.

I'm not going to make this easy for her, I want to make her say it.

The line is silent apart from the rasping, unsteady breaths coming from my mother.

Eventually she speaks. Her voice has a forced flatness, like she has squeezed any emotion that she might be feeling out of it. "You've talked to her about Jordan? About Bridlington? Have you told her about Chester?"

A bitter smile settles on my lips.

I knew it.

I knew that my mother would go back to that.

I knew that eventually she would dig everything up again. It's dead and buried, and that's where I plan to leave it.

"I don't want to talk to you about what I discuss with my psychiatrist," I say. "I'm sure she knows everything that I've ever told to anyone else. She has my file. I don't have to rehash everything again. She's going to help me get better, not make me feel worse."

Now it's Mum's turn to sigh. I know she will have caught my implication that she is, in fact, doing just that: making things worse.

This conversation isn't going the way I'd hoped. All I wanted was comfort.

"Can't you just..." I begin the sentence, but I don't know how to finish it.

"What?" She snaps at me; she's tired, tired of me. How unlucky she must be to lose her perfect son, and be left with her fuck-up of a daughter.

"Never mind," I say. "I'm going to go now."

"Beck-" she starts, but before she finishes saying my name, I end the call.

After I've hung up, I lie on my belly, pressing my face down into the bed. I could cry. Maybe you would. Maybe any normal person would. I could, but I don't. I feel frustrated and angry, rather than sad.

What I said to Mum was true. I assume that Brightside knows everything that I told Balliol, that there must be some way of them sharing information between them, in a professional way. I gave my consent for that info-sharing to happen, right at the start, right when I started to see Balliol. She told me that everything that we discussed was confidential, unless she needed to discuss something with another professional, or unless I revealed something that implied harm to myself or to another person. Perhaps that's one of the reasons that I was so reluctant to start engaging with Balliol. I didn't want to say the wrong thing; I didn't want to say too much.

Anything you say may be given in evidence.

You can't make something out of nothing. I knew that if I didn't say anything, my words couldn't be analysed. When I did start to open up, I was careful. I told her what she wanted to hear, and everyone seemed a lot happier. Not me though; I was the same messed-up kid. I still am, nothing has changed.

Chapter Twenty-Five

They don't keep Michaela in for long. It's only two days later; I've just finished checking my mailbox in the lobby, and I'm about to head back upstairs when I almost run into her. Long, bright red hair; savage, angry bruises on her face. I notice, while I'm staring at her, how much the colour of her bruising looks like jewels. Emerald, amethyst, amber; it's almost beautiful.

I'm not sure if she will say anything to me. We don't know each other really. I don't think she would even recognise me if we walked past each other on campus. We would probably do just that: walk past each other. We have no reason to stop and say 'hello'. She's Heidi's friend, or more than that, whatever they are.

I nod at her, and she nods back. That's it.

I have some junk mail, but there's nothing important. It's what I expected. There's no one that is likely to write to me. It's not Mum's style, and who else do I really have? If Jordan...if what happened hadn't happened...I can imagine he and I writing old-school traditional letters to each other. Pen and paper, maybe postcards, every week.

Here's the latest.

Guess what happened?

Little drawings in the margins; Everything could have been different, but it's not.

I go up the stairs, up to the flat, up to my room. Sure enough, there's Heidi.

"I just saw Michaela in the lobby," I say. "Is she okay now?"

Heidi nods, but doesn't smile.

"What's up?"

She's standing by the entrance to the kitchen, and before she speaks, she flops onto the sofa and lets out a sigh. It's melodramatic, but under the circumstances I don't flinch.

"She doesn't remember what happened, not clearly, but..." she says.

I'm worried now. I sit on the other sofa, hands on my lap, trying not to tremble, and I ask, "What?"

Heidi looks at me, tears filling her eyes. She says, "She thinks it might not have been an accident."

"Not what? How?"

"It's a bit of a blur, but she said she thinks someone might have pushed her." Heidi starts to cry, her face contorting into an ugly, scrunched mess.

"Fuck," I say, because I don't know how else to respond. "Really?"

"Yeah." Heidi tries her best to speak between her sobs. "She remembers that she was on the landing, she had her bag, she turned around and then someone came out of our flat. In a hurry."

"Our flat? *OUR* flat? Who? What? Fuck." My sloth-paced brain patches the pieces together. "Listen, I don't know if Cally told you, but I think someone has been following me. You know Security came up here…"

"Yeah, and Micki went to Security too. They said no one else has been into the building. No one that doesn't live here." She pulls a face and groans. "I don't know…"

"That's what they told me too. I think the CCTV must be screwed. They can't keep saying the same thing. I mean I just believed them when they told me that but…maybe…it's either fucked or they are completely useless."

I try to think of the name of the guy I spoke to who wasn't Fats or Jack.

"She's not sure though, so she doesn't want to push it. Maybe she just tripped." Heidi wipes at her eyes. I haven't moved towards her to comfort her. Perhaps that's what she expected, but I'm not very good at this sort of thing; I don't deal well with emotion.

I understand Michaela's uncertainty

though. Uncertainty is one of my best friends, we spend a lot of time together. It's one of my worst enemies really, of course; I hate it. I can't shake those feelings though, and I understand them well enough to sympathise with Michaela, at least a little bit.

"Just in case though," I say. "Please make sure the flat door is always locked. I mean, I know you probably do, but…"

She nods. "No, sure. Really, yeah." We both pause. "It's probably nothing. It's fine."

I'm not certain of anything anymore.

"So, you and her…?" I half-ask the question and she half-answers with a shrug.

"I don't know," she says. "I've never…" Her cheeks blossom with a deep flush of red. It's cute; it makes her look kind-of innocent.

"Never been with a girl? Never liked girls that way?" I know the questions will make her uncomfortable, but I want to know, so I ask anyway.

She shrugs again.

"Either." She shifts position, tries not to look at me. Her tears have stopped now, at least that's something.

"It's okay not to know," I say. "What you like, I mean, to not know what you want. It's okay to be yourself, and do what feels right."

That's what Jordan told me. Those were his exact words, or at least the words as I remember them. I told him about the feelings that I had started to have, because there was no one else that I could tell. No one else would have understood me, or listened to me without judging. Jordan made me feel that I *could* be myself, and that I *should*.

Heidi looks at me.

"Thanks, Becky."

She smiles, and it is beautiful. Her teeth are perfect. She has a gorgeous, pearly-white perfectly straight smile, I wish mine were like that. I wish I could smile more. Her lips are painted with raspberry coloured gloss, sweet and shiny. I wonder what it's like to kiss her. I wonder if she tastes as sweet as that gloss looks.

Heidi speaks again. "I don't know if she..."

I nod. She doesn't have to explain. "Maybe she doesn't know either, but the two of you can work through this together." I'm full of good advice.

On the surface, this is the most honest exchange I have had since I moved here. Underneath, I wish that Michaela didn't exist. I wish I hadn't lived the kind of life that had turned me into the fucked-up shell of a girl that I am now. I wish and I wish, but wishes don't come true. Not for people like me.

Chapter Twenty-Six

Heidi goes over to see Michaela, and I decide I've had enough company for one day. I head back into my room. I'm about to start reading a book. I pull it from the drawer in the table next to me, and my eyes pause at the sight of the bottle of Jack Daniels. I like to look at it, even though I've never touched a drop. It was Jordan's favourite. This was his. I took it as a kind of sick memento, I guess. It reminds me of him, it reminds me of that night, and it reminds me never to drink again. I slam the drawer closed.

I settle onto my bed, and reach to draw the curtain, and then stop. I'm still holding the thick, dull slub, but my body has frozen.

I can see someone. Someone watching, someone staring. They are in exactly the same place as I saw them before, next to the tree. They are looking up at me in exactly the same way.

Oh fuck no. Not this again.

Once, I could pass off as chance, but we are way beyond that now.

I am awake, I am not imagining this, there is no doubt in my mind.

I'm ready this time. My phone is within reach, and I grab it, never taking my eyes off the figure. I lift my phone and take a photograph, and then a second, just in case. The person down there must have seen what I'm doing because they immediately turn and start to walk away. Just a casual stroll; they don't run off, like someone who's been caught doing something wrong, they literally just walk. I stop for a few seconds, trying to decide what to do.

Fuck it. I'm going down there. I need to know who this is. I've got to find out why they are doing this to me.

Everything has been a mess, a clouded jumble in my mind that I couldn't put together, but suddenly, it all seems clear. This person. I wasn't sure the first time, I am rarely certain of anything, but now it feels as though a fog has lifted. This person. Whoever this person is, they are responsible. The certainty feels like relief, as though there is almost an end in sight. Instead of feeling anger or fear, I have a rush of happiness that comes from the thought that perhaps, just maybe, I can deal with this, and finally start to move forward.

I scramble from the bed, yank on my boots, and scoop my jacket off the peg, pulling it on as I run out. I race through the living room, where Eamon and Cally are sitting, watching TV.

"You okay?" Cally shouts, but I don't stop to answer. I wave, though, and I'm smiling as I go.

I'm out of the door and on the stairs, taking them two at a time. I suddenly remember Michaela's 'accident' and slow myself a little. There's no one around to push me, but it would be ironic if I fell down on my way to meet my destiny.

I shove the entrance door, and shoot around the side of the building. The paths are icy, so I keep to the grass, heading for the tree, all the time focused on where I'm going. My heart is beating out of my chest.

Of course, when I get to the tree they have already gone. I stop, look in the direction I saw them walk, trying to pick out a figure moving ahead.

Too late, I think. *Too late*.

I put my hands onto my thighs and bend, lowering my head.

Fuck. Fuck. Fuck.

I stand and pull up my hood. It's so cold outside now. I can't just stand here; I have to keep moving. I look up, and I start walking dead ahead. The person had started their slow pace off in this direction; it's the only lead I have. I can't lose them; this has to end.

As I get past the back of East, I have a better

view of the campus. It's flat out here, but there are still thick, heavy trees dotted around. I see a flash of movement in my peripheral vision. I centre in on it, focussing, trying to see what it is, trying to see if it's him, her, whoever.

It is a figure. My heart almost stops when I see them. It's definitely a person. They have their hands in their pockets, and they are walking slowly, looking at the ground. It doesn't seem right; there's no urgency, no attempt to get away unnoticed.

Unless they want this, I think. *Unless they want me to see them. Unless they want me to follow them and catch them.*

The thought gives me goosebumps. I feel all the tiny hairs on my arms bristle against my sleeves. If they want this, they must have a plan. What's my plan? What exactly am I going to say when I catch up with them? I have no idea. All I know is that my life has been a nightmare, and I want it to end.

I don't think they've seen me, but I have a deep, unshakeable feeling that they know I am here, following. The figure turns off on a path to the right. If they'd kept going, they would have reached the tower blocks, and the car park. I could have believed they were a visitor to campus, lost, no ill-intentions. Instead, they're travelling towards the fields that stretch along the south-east of campus. They are heading out into the open; they certainly are not trying to hide.

I lag back, try to keep a tree in the line of vision between me and them, but also making sure I don't lose sight. If I can see them, they can see me. I don't want to be too obvious. I want them to think they lost me. I'm trying to sneak, but I have no experience at this; I'm clueless and clumsy.

There's a slight dip at the edge of the field, and a break in visual contact as the figure moves downhill. I'm gripped by the fear that I might lose them.

Shit shit shit.

I quicken my pace, less concerned about being seen, more concerned about keeping sight of the figure. I clip the top of the mound, and freeze in my track.

There's a bench, halfway down the hill, by the edge of the path, and there's someone sitting on it.

I can't see anyone else around. There's no one else here. It must be them.

I stand, statue still for a few seconds, trying to think. This is it. I finally have them here in front of me. I wish I had thought of a plan; I have nothing. I feel surprisingly calm, despite my galloping heart rate and the massive dose of adrenaline racing through me. I am aware of those things, but I feel in control. I take a final look around; it's just me and this person. I was right when I first saw them, they are around my height and build. Apart from that, I couldn't tell you anything else. All I can see is the hooded shape on the bench.

One thing I didn't account for is that it's starting to get pretty dark now, especially out here away from the campus buildings. I don't want to be out here much longer. I want to talk to this person, and put an end to this.

I take a breath, and commit.

"Hey," I shout, not really knowing what I'm going to say yet. I'll have to play it by ear.

I start to bridge the gap between us.

They don't turn around.

They don't move.

"Hey!" I shout louder, I walk closer.

Nothing.

Fuck's sake, I mutter beneath my breath.

This game isn't fun.

I jog the last few yards, and stop behind them.

"Hey," I say, quietly and calmly.

Nothing.

"We need to talk about this," I say. "Who are you? Why the fuck are you stalking me?"

The figure pats the bench next to them but says nothing. They don't even turn to look at me.

Really??

I sigh, cold, exhausted and sick of this shit. I walk around to the bench.

The face is obscured by the person's hoodie. When I sit down, she turns to look at me, and I recognise her instantly, even though it's been two years since I last saw her.

I know who she is. And I know why she is here.

Chapter Twenty-Seven

As soon as I sit, she spits in my face. I wasn't expecting that. I recoil instantly, almost tumbling backward, off the bench.

I've made a big mistake, following her, coming here. I know that already, but I am here. We are here, and we have to end this.

I can make out the lights of Lake House in the distance. If I get up and start running, if I need to, I could get to the security office, I could get to -

I don't finish my thought, because she swings a fist out at me. I try to get up, pushing my hands down on the cold wood, pressing my feet into the hardened mud of the ground. She pulls me back down, her little fists fast on my hoodie.

"Sit the fuck down. You wanted to talk," she says. "'*We need to talk about this*'." Her tone mocks me. "I've been waiting for the right time. I've been waiting for two years to get you away from your family, to get you alone. You only ever left the house to go to your fucking therapy sessions." Her face is an angry snarl. She launches a fist at my face, and it connects this time. "Crazy fucking bitch."

Fuck, it hurts. I've never been in a fight

before, no one has ever hit me. All the shit that has ever been thrown at me has been verbal, emotional, and personal. No one ever bothered to punch me. Fuck.

I try again to get to my feet, and she grabs onto me, clawing and dragging at me.

She's come all this way to stalk me, rattling books around a library, probably breaking into my room, and she's calling me crazy? Now that she is here, now that this is happening, I believe everything that my messed-up mind had been doubting. She has been the cause of all the things that have happened, she must have been.

She's dangerous, I know it. I need to get away.

My eyes dart around, but she has hold of me and I can't push her off.

She starts talking, and I wish she would stop. I wish she wasn't here, I wish I wasn't here, I wish I had imagined all of it.

"You shouldn't have even been there. You were sixteen years old. You shouldn't have been drinking. You shouldn't have been in the club in the first place."

I wasn't meant to be there of course. I was sixteen. Two years shy of the legal entry age for that club, but Jordan knew a kid who made fake IDs, and he hooked me up.

Jordan always came through for me, every time.

I'd told Mum and Dad that I would be at a friend's house, and I think they were just relieved that I finally had a friend close enough to invite me over.

Was it worth it? The gig was amazing, it was everything I thought it would be. I had promised Jordan that I only needed the ID for entry, and that I wouldn't drink, but when I was in there...well, I guess I got carried away. I thought I'd give it a try, go to the bar, order a drink, see if they'd serve me. Of course, they knew I must have been ID-checked at the door, so the barman measured me out a Jack and Coke and pushed it towards me.

It turned out I liked it. I had four more.

I'd never drunk alcohol before, so you can imagine the effect.

Jennie swings out at me and I dodge. Jennie; of course it would be Jennie. I underestimated her. I underestimated her relationship with Jordan, and I underestimated just how messed up she was by losing him. How very fucking ironic. If there was one person that she should have been able to talk to, who could have understood what she had lost, it should have been me. We never spoke though, not even at the funeral. I didn't want anything to do with her. I resented her when Jordan was alive, for all the time that he spent with her, when he should have been with me.

As if reading my mind, she says, "Everything always had to be about you. You. The centre of everything."

Despite her fury, she's not shouting at me. That makes it even more scary. She is in control, and she knows exactly what she is doing.

My eyes are desperately scanning for the glowing flashlights of Jack or Fats in the distance.

"No one's coming to save you, you fucking bitch."

She lashes out and her fist connects with my cheek again. It pounds against the same place she hit the first time, and my face feels fragile. The pain burns at my skin. I try to hit back, but my arms flail uselessly.

Jordan came to collect me at half-past eleven. My curfew was midnight and it was a twenty-minute drive. We agreed the extra ten minutes just to be on the safe side. Safe. I wish we had been.

I was outside the front of the club, when he pulled up beside me at dead on eleven-thirty. He knew when I opened the car door that I had been drinking.

"Becky, why?" he said. "You're going to be in so much trouble."

"I love you," I said. My brain floated with alcohol and happiness.

"Fucking hell. I love you too, Becks, but...damn, what are you doing?"

I leaned across the car, the gear stick jamming into my gut, and put my arms around him. I remember that I gave him such a big, sloppy kiss on his cheek that despite his annoyance, he started to laugh. I couldn't bear him being mad at me, I had to soften him.

"When we get back, say you have a headache, or you're tired or something. Go straight upstairs. I'll cover for you," he said. He was always the one with the plans.

"You're the best," I slurred, and I meant it.

He was the best; he was everything.

I was elated, but as he set off, I started to feel nauseated.

I'm tearing at Jennie's hand, trying to release her grip, and get her off me. She's strong, I'll give her that.

"I loved him. He was my world. And he's gone because of you." She keeps talking, and she keeps throwing punches at me.

Jennie, Jennie, Jennie.

I didn't even realise that she and Jordan had been so serious. They'd been a couple since the beginning of college, for two years nearly. That wasn't long enough to be so serious, so young was it? What do I know about it? I've never loved anyone. Not in that way.

I loved Jordan. I loved him so much. I keep saying it, I know, but right now, that's the thought that keeps surfacing in my head.

She hits me again, and I'm suddenly out of her grip, as I fall to the floor. That was a hard one, and it winded me, knocked me off balance.

Jordan drove us through the town, and out onto the country roads that led to our village. He was a careful driver. Whatever anyone says, he was always careful. He'd passed his test about six months earlier, first time, of course. He did everything to the letter, and he did everything well. That was pretty frustrating sometimes, seeing as I was the little sister that couldn't live up to his example, but that was Jordan: too perfect.

"Put your foot down! I don't want to be late back!" I was shouting, stupid drunk.

"I'm going at the speed limit already." His voice stayed calm. He was trying to get me back in line. "Open your window. Sober up a bit."

I reached over and clicked the stereo on. He kept his eyes on the road, but I saw just a flicker of a look in my direction, like a warning shot.

"How was your night, Beck?" He was doing his best to calm me down, get me back on level ground before we got home. He was always doing his best.

I scramble to my feet; this is my chance.

"Help me! Someone! Help!" I yell so loud that my throat burns.

"No one is going to help you," Jennie says. She almost laughs. "No one."

I start to run, and she runs after me. I focus on the light of Lake House, work out the quickest way around the water to get to it. It's dark now, and the ground is uneven. I don't want to trip, and end up back on the floor; I don't want to do anything that gives her the edge again. I have to run, but I have to be careful.

Our song came on the radio

You and me...

We're on the path...

We're on a roll...

and I reached out and turned it up. I was always careful not to get in his way when he was driving, but I reached over. I cranked it up and he glanced at me, just out of the corner of his eye and he said, "Becky Bear. Turn it down. It's late. People live here."

The more I flail to escape her grip, the tighter it becomes. She's dragging me now. Her hands tight around my upper arms, walking backwards, hauling me like I'm a sack of flour. I try to dig my feet into the ground. I'm trying to do something, trying to do anything to resist her traction, to stop her from pulling me.

She's got me though.

She's got me and there's nothing I can do.

"No one lives here," I said.

We were on an open stretch of road, just before the dual carriageway. He was driving fast, below the speed limit, but fast.

"It's distracting me. I can't concentrate." His voice became agitated. I was irritating him, I knew. I hated it when that happened. Sometimes I was

too much for him. He tried to tolerate me, but if I wasn't his sister, he would have told me to fuck off, I know.

He moved his hand to click the volume dial down; I turned it back up and our hands tangled. He was batting me away and he swerved and

And...

She's taking me towards the water. I kick and I throw my arms in desperate punches. Somehow, I can't connect. I can't do anything that makes her stop.

"Please," I say. It comes out like a squeal, a wounded sow-noise. I don't recognise it as my voice. I feel lost. I'm fucking terrified.

"Shut the fuck up."

She stops for a moment, still gripping me, and aims a kick into my ribs. A searing pain rips through my torso.

Fuck.

Fuck, fuck, fuck.

"Please, stop." What else can I say?

She kicks me again, harder.

"Jennie," I say, in a stretched, anguished moan of a word. "Jennie, please."

I saw him lying there, metal cradling his body. His head smashed on the steering wheel, the blood splattered over the driver's window, over the crazy paving cracks in the windscreen. His mouth was frothing red foam, something had gone through one of his lungs. It was a rib, fractured and popped out of place. I learned that later of course. It's not something you can see. It's not something I wanted to think about.

I read somewhere that if you're attacked you should try to reason with your attacker. If not, then aim for the eyes, or the genitals. Kick 'em in the balls. I never expected to be attacked by someone a couple of years older than myself, and much the same size. Regardless of that, she's strong. She's too strong.

"Jennie. You don't need to do this. What do you want?" The words are painful. I can't breathe properly. I think something might be broken. My chest is on fire and I'm rasping.

She kicks me again and I howl.

His eyes were open, but he was struggling to keep them that way. I could see his pain; I could almost feel it, but I couldn't feel my own, not then, not as it was happening. I was driven by my instincts to get myself free, and get out of there. That's all I could feel: that force, that primal drive.

"I loved him too," I manage to say. "Jennie, I loved him."

"You killed him. You fucking bitch. You killed him." Her venomous hatred fills every word.

We are on the move again. I can taste blood. Every breath burns. The pain is almost unbearable. She drags me, and my broken body bumps over the frozen ground. Down the hill, she keeps pulling, and I keep moving. There's nothing I can do.

When we get to the side of the lake, she stops, and pushes me in the chest with the palm of her hand. My head hits the ground, but it's not as hard here, the damp of the lake has softened it to a numbing mud. It still hurts like a bitch.

I try to find the breath to say her name again. If I can reason with her, appeal to her somehow, perhaps she will stop this. My eyes dart along the horizon, searching out any sign of anyone else around the lake. There's no one. The security office is within view, but out of range of my shouts, even if I could shout now. I'm winded and wounded and, oh fuck -

I looked all around in desperation. I was looking for any kind of weak spot in the wreckage, searching for somewhere I could get in to him, to do something useful for him. But I couldn't. I couldn't see anything. I tried. I did. I tried.

She grabs me by the hair and pulls my head. I know what's coming next before she even starts to move me. I make one final desperate attempt to release myself, trying to headbutt her legs, trying to make her unsteady; maybe I can topple her.

It doesn't work. I can't connect. I'm so fucking useless. Instead, she aims another kick into my gut, and I crumple.

She pulls my head up, and in one swooping movement dunks it below the freezing surface of the lake. I hadn't taken a breath first and the shock of the stabbing cold makes me draw a mouthful of water. I thrash my arms, trying to hit her, trying to grab her, trying to stop her; failing, failing, failing.

It's a swift dunking. She pulls my head back up, and I swear she is laughing. I cough, choke, try to breathe, cough some more.

"You didn't try to help him. You kicked open your door, and you climbed out. You looked at him lying there and you left him." She brings her face down, level with mine, and spits the words out.

"Wh-what?" I stutter. I should be using this time to breathe, or to fight, but instead I ask the question.

"If you had tried to pull him out, he'd be alive now. You had time to save yourself. You should have saved him. You should have fucking tried."

She hasn't let go of my hair, her fingers are tangle-tied in it, gripping me.

"Help! Someone fucking help!" I manage to yell, using the last of my energy. Then I look at her. I wonder how long she has planned this, how much hatred has built inside her, how far she is prepared to go. "Jennie...stop..."

She pushes my head back into the stinging-cold water.

.

I got out. I did. He didn't. He wanted me to. He wanted me to be safe. There was nothing I could do.

There was nothing I could do.
My brother.
Jordan.
I left him.

As I clamp my mouth shut, fighting against the pain of the cold and the unbearable, insensible urge to gulp the water into my lungs, I can hear the muffled sound of her voice.

"Bitch...killed him...love...bitch..."

It's all I can make out. She's held me under for longer this time. I can't hold on. I need to breathe. Everything starts to turn black -

All I thought about in the days and months afterwards was his face. He watched me climb out of the car. He knew there was no hope for him. He knew it was over. Every time I closed my eyes, I saw it.

Every time I tried to sleep, I was haunted by the fact: it was my fault. He died because of me.

She pulls my head out of the water.

"Crazy bitch," she finishes saying. "Look at you. I thought you'd fight harder, you know. I thought this would be more difficult. It's easy though isn't it?" Her voice is so steady, she's so stable. Her calmness terrifies me more than anything.

She's in control. She knows what she is doing, and she is doing this. She is doing it.

"No," I shout, I scream, use everything I have left, every last shred of my reserves to get this word out, but the word is useless.

Water.
Freezing.
Water.
Thrash.
Water.
Push.
Water.

That song. Jordan's face. I left him. I left him.

Water.
Water.
Darkness.

You and me.
You and me.
You

Epilogue

The search for Rebecca Braithwaite didn't begin until four days after she went missing. Her body wasn't discovered until three weeks later.

Rebecca's tutor, Professor Sophie Dean, raised the alarm after the Wessex University student missed a series of lectures, and her flatmates were unable to obtain a response from her room.

In 2018, Rebecca was a passenger in a car accident that led to the death of her brother, Jordan. Following the tragic loss of her only sibling, she received psychiatric care as an outpatient of renowned specialist Doctor Stephanie Balliol.

Doctor Balliol was unavailable for comment.

Rebecca was plagued by persistent insomnia, which affected her concentration and led to violent mood swings.

"I think she got tired in so many ways," said her mother, Amy Braithwaite of Harborough, West Yorkshire. "She never slept properly after Jordan's death. She was snappy and always on edge. I tried my best to support her, but nothing seemed to get through."

"She blamed herself for what happened with her brother," said Jennie Milton, Jordan's long-term girlfriend. "We all tried to support her and help her to see that it wasn't her fault, but she carried that guilt around with her. Jordan and Rebecca adored each other."

Ms. Braithwaite had a history of violence and severe mental health issues, dating back to her early teens. She was hospitalised at the age of fifteen for a two-week period in a secure unit in Bridlington, after she strangled the family's ginger tomcat, Chester in an unmotivated attack.

"She loved Chester," said her mother. "She and Jordan worshipped the animal. It was always on one of their laps. I don't know why she did what she did. I'll never understand it. She was always such a peaceful child; it was like something in her just snapped."

"It was unfortunate that she never sought further psychiatric help when she started University. The move away from home, away from her family, was obviously stressful to her, and had a grave impact on her already fragile mental state," said her GP, Doctor Fisher.

Miss Braithwaite had struggled to make friends

after starting university a month prior to her death. Her flatmates rarely saw her leave her room, and knew little about the quiet, introverted student.

"She never mentioned self-harm or gave any indication that she might commit suicide," said her flatmate, Caroline Clarkson. "I knew that she had some issues. She had trouble with insomnia, and she seemed quite paranoid...always saying she thought that someone was out to get her. I thought that she was out of touch with reality."

Rebecca's body was found after a SCUBA team organised by Wessex police force searched the lake on Wessex University campus. The body was in poor condition, but it was possible for the police to confirm that Miss Braithwaite had weighed herself down before entering the water. Her rucksack was filled with heavyweight hardback books.

"The books appeared to be connected to an article she was writing for one of her assignments on the effects of insomnia. There was also a psychological thriller, the genre she enjoyed reading."

The textbooks had been checked out from the university's library earlier in term. The hardback was from the student's own personal collection.

A spokesperson from the university said, "Rebecca had contacted campus security several times in the weeks leading up to her tragic death. She was clearly a disturbed young lady, with a vivid imagination. Her mental health issues had not been disclosed to the university in her application, and we understand that she failed to reach out for support. We have resources and assistance available to all students that require them."

Cally copy and pasted the helpline number into the end of the document, ran the spellcheck on her assignment, and saved the file. What had anyone ever really known about Becky?

Dear Reader,

Thank you for choosing "I Can't Sleep".

If you have enjoyed reading this book, please consider leaving a review on Amazon and/or Goodreads. Your reviews help other readers to find my books.

If you would like to find out more about me, and get information about upcoming publications, you can find my website at jerowney.com and sign up to my mailing list.

I'm also on social media.
Twitter: http://twitter.com/jerowneywriter
Instagram: http://www.instagram.com/jerowneywriter
Facebook: http://www.facebook.com/jerowneywriter

See you there!

JE Rowney

Made in the USA
Monee, IL
06 March 2025

13560376R00154